## "Paid-for kisses aren't exactly what I need..."

Easy Ride seemed to contemplate Kirby's admission.

"Then I'll stop the clock, kiss you for ten minutes, then we'll resume with the paid-for session. How does that sound?"

All of a sudden she was hyperaware of their proximity, how utterly strong and protective his arm felt around her, how his sensual mouth would feel while exploring her own, if she wanted it.

And she definitely wanted.

"Why would you do that?" she asked.

"I want to kiss you. Why else?"

Before she could overanalyze it, he pressed his mouth against hers and tenderly nudged her lips apart with his tongue.

She wanted to consume him, as he had begun to consume her.

For the next several minutes, her feelings swung from one end of the emotional spectrum to the other—from being convinced that he enjoyed the deep and intimate kisses as much as ~~sh~~ wondering whether this w~~as~~ job duty, then back

As Kirby struggled "convinced," some~~o~~ them.

Dear Reader,

I've always been curious about what goes on behind closed doors. Especially when they're unmarked and belong to discreet businesses. I have stepped behind such a door and entered a world where couples claim an enclave or a sofa and get to know each other better. Sometimes a *lot* better. That club, which shall remain nameless, was the inspiration for this book.

In *Easy Ride*, I'll take you behind the unmarked door of a referral-only club where gorgeous men are paid to salve the emotional wounds of women. Where Kirby, an undercover reporter, meets Adam—a male escort with a heart of gold beneath those amazing pecs and equestrian tattoos. Of course, Kirby needs the type of comfort these men offer even more than she needs a story. Adam's heart, and his past, need mending, as well. And Kirby is just the woman to do it.

I hope you'll fall in love with Kirby and Adam as deeply as I have. Whatever you do, keep opening doors.

Enjoy!

*Suzanne Ruby*

# Suzanne Ruby

---

## *Easy Ride*

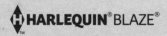
HARLEQUIN® BLAZE®

Recycling programs
for this product may
not exist in your area.

ISBN-13: 978-0-373-79971-8

Easy Ride

**HARLEQUIN**®
www.Harlequin.com

**Printed in U.S.A.**

**Suzanne Ruby**'s writing journey was once as eclectic as the books that grace her shelves. What began as a desire to craft romantic short stories evolved into writing literary fiction, personal essays and poetry. Her journey came full circle when she joined Romance Writers of America and got down to the business—and the pleasure—of writing novel-length contemporary romance. And she has never looked back.

When she isn't making her heroes and heroines work hard and play even harder, Suzanne is being mercilessly bossed around by her and her husband's alpha-female German Shepherd at their home in Houston, Texas...and enjoying every minute of it!

Visit her at suzanneruby.com.

For David and Bella—my special angels.

## Acknowledgments

Many thanks to Sandra Bretting, my critique partner since the beginning of our writing journey.

To my genre BFFs, Meta Carroll, Robin Gianna, Sarah Andre and Lark Brennan.

And my lifesaver, Perry Jackson.

To my parents, Martha and Bobby, for their unconditional love and encouragement. And my husband, Jeff, for knowing when to be there for me and when to leave me alone and let me write.

Also, special thanks to my wonderful agent, Linda Scalissi, and my amazing editor, Dana Grimaldi, for their gentle, brilliant guidance.

# _1_

KIRBY MONTGOMERY ADJUSTED the long blond wig that seemed to be crawling off her scalp with each step. It was almost as if the ridiculous thing were warning her not to follow through with this supremely bad idea.

As if she needed to be warned.

She'd come to this club specifically in search of "bad." Her reputation depended on it.

Three young men dressed in Wrangler jeans, tight T-shirts and cowboy hats puffed menthols and sipped longnecks near the front entrance of Deep in the Heart, but they paused long enough to gift Kirby with an appreciative once-over.

Ordinarily, she'd welcome such validation. But validation wasn't what she was after tonight.

She clenched the valet ticket as she would a set of winning lottery numbers. She needed that piece of paper—to claim her Volvo at the end of the night and to access the part of this joint where the real action took place.

The first step of the process was a no-brainer: present the valet ticket to the gentleman directly inside the door and say "I have a reservation and here's my number."

Problem was, as soon as the phrase spilled from her

lips, she wasn't sure whether she had nailed the sequence. At least, not until the doorman texted someone, returned her ticket and said, "You're good to go."

Damn dyslexia. Even though she'd all but conquered the beast, it still had the power to trip her up and strip her confidence bare.

Step two proved to be a bit more challenging: locate the red door in the back of the club. That meant maneuvering around the dance floor, past the tables overflowing with people.

The scents of beer, drugstore perfume and good-ole-boy arrogance made her stomach roil as she dodged the drunks and the dreamers who came to the club to either get laid or find true love.

She'd almost made it around the first curve when one of the drunken dreamers grabbed her arm.

"Dance with me, darlin'," he said as the deejay cued up Alan Jackson's "Mercury Blues."

The valet ticket slithered from her hand as he twirled her onto the dance floor. She immediately lost sight of it beneath the trampling of boots.

Her own feet tangled beneath her, and her emotions became tied in impossible knots as she tried to get oriented. The whole club spun round and round in all its wood-beamed, high-ceilinged, taxidermy-deer-headed glory. She couldn't even make out the face of her partner, who, to his credit, maintained an abundance of patience with his two-left-footed partner.

Then again, this was his fault for assuming she could dance, much less wanted to.

She somehow made it through the song without breaking the guy's foot or crushing his ego with the well-chosen words she'd managed to squelch. Once safely grounded on the sidelines, she exhausted every drop of remaining focus to identify a landmark.

Thank God, she'd somehow ended up about where she started, logistically.

Emotionally, the whole unplanned two-step had wrecked her. She couldn't even bear to think about the physical damage. Was her wig still on her head? If so, how bad did it look?

She reached up. Fortunately, the beast had remained reasonably intact. She scanned the dance floor for the ticket. What was her number anyway? Was it 181, or 818? Or neither? As she was about to go up front and beg for help, someone tapped her shoulder.

*Not again.*

She spun around and said, "No, I do *not* want to dance."

As soon as she saw the man's face, she wished she could take it back. Sure, it was dark in this place, but that didn't shroud certain details, such as the pale blue tint of his eyes. It sure as hell didn't detract from the sensual shape of his lips. And damn, he looked good in a black Stetson.

At such proximity, the part of her that had been refused, rejected and turned away reawakened with unexpected force. It tugged at her like an iron hand, clad in satin. Forceful and sensual, all at once.

"I don't recall asking," he said. "I believe you dropped this."

He produced the ticket, along with a curious half smile and a tip of the hat.

*Oh.* Of course he wasn't going to ask her to dance. Why would he?

She accepted the ticket and held it up to the only light she could find. It had somehow survived the stampede, even though boot scuffs and indentions had scarred the surface and ripped the edges.

Her number—181. She was almost certain.

By the time she thought to thank the man, he'd disappeared into the crowd. Just as well. She had work to do.

After dodging more easygoing cowboys, she finally located the red door.

The no-turning-back-once-you're-inside door.

She positioned her purse so that the miniature camera, disguised as a zipper bauble, pointed forward.

Moments after punching her valet number into a keypad next to the frame, the door buzzed open and the world changed from honky-tonk to urban lounge.

The only design thread connecting the two different businesses was the cowhide rug beneath her feet, though this one was black and white. Colorless, like everything else around her. Like the stark white podium with only an iPad on top, the glossy white IKEA-inspired cabinet and the white semitransparent scrim of fabric that separated the entry from a darkened room beyond.

An antique chandelier overhead added a touch of romance, but the bulbs were much too bright. All of a sudden she felt overexposed. And far too obvious.

Time to lose the wig. No one would recognize her anyway. Nor would they recognize her name, since she remained eternally stuck behind the scenes at the television station. Shivering in the shadow of Seth Wainwright's reporter-slash-celebrity ego. But this assignment had the power to change all of that.

She deep-sixed the wig in a tall black trash can situated in the corner, then unleashed her long brunette hair from the strict confines of the elastic ponytail holder, which she slipped around her wrist.

Before she had time to retrieve a comb from her purse, a man parted the scrim and approached.

He looked as though he'd been interrupted in the middle of getting dressed. Or perhaps undressed. The white dress shirt had been unbuttoned to reveal his tan, smooth six-pack. That, along with the gray wool pants, black leather belt and shiny dress shoes, suggested business and pleasure mixed quite beautifully here.

He wasn't the man she had booked, based on the minimal facial features revealed in the portal photos. Not to mention, this one had blond, rather than borderline black, hair. Furthermore, he looked much too tame.

If nothing else, The Deep's website was an excellent example of male objectification at its finest.

"You must be Kirby."

And just like that, she felt as if she'd been stripped naked.

"How do you know my name? I thought anonymity was guaranteed." In fact, she was sure of it.

The man remained gorgeously stoic as he walked around the desk and typed something into the iPad.

"You provided that info when you signed up. But don't worry. I'm the only one who knows. To everyone else, you're a number."

*I've been a number before.*

"I'll need your valet ticket," he continued. "You'll exit out back when you're done, and we'll pull your car around. We find most ladies like the extra privacy."

She handed him the sad shrapnel of paper. "Sorry. Turns out the ticket isn't very good on the dance floor."

No response. Not even a smile. He simply turned his attention back to the iPad.

At this angle, his profile and the depth of his concentration seemed familiar.

"Have we met before?" she asked.

Might as well get it out in the open now. Otherwise, her cover could be blown mid-assignment. Better to forfeit the story before it began and cover the oil-and-gas scandal instead, even though this was the story she wanted. Make that needed. On so many levels.

"Not that I'm aware," he said without so much as looking up. His fingers continued to glide across the screen.

A few more moments passed, but the familiarity wouldn't allow her to drop the subject.

"What's *your* name?" she asked.

He glanced up from the tablet and evaluated her with the greenest eyes she'd ever seen. Now those she definitely didn't recognize, which was somewhat reassuring.

"Fabian."

*Yeah, right.*

While she waited for Fabian, or whoever he was, to finish his task, she imagined what moniker she would have chosen.

The answer was easy. She'd been compared to Sandra Bullock at least a dozen times. Except, her own eyes were an ever-changing hazel instead of rich, movie-star brown. And her teeth were far from perfect, with both cuspids slightly overlapping their neighboring incisors. She'd shared that quirky trait with her mom. To correct it would mean losing her all over again.

"First time here, I see," Fabian said.

"I guess that makes me a virgin. I don't mean I'm a *virgin* virgin, I meant—"

"You booked Easy Ride to pop your cherry. Excellent choice."

She gulped. But the knot of self-consciousness in her throat didn't budge, and she could barely speak around it.

"So I'm paying for...*sex*?"

This story was going to be easier to wrap up than she had originally thought. She'd barely crafted a lede beyond something like "The Deep, an underground male escort service nestled within the popular country dance hall Deep in the Heart, is allegedly serving up more than longnecks and a shoulder to cry on. It is suspected as a front for prostitution."

"We're not that kind of club." He punctuated the straightforward defense with a cordial smile.

"I was kidding. I crack stupid jokes when I'm nervous."

She flashed her full-on genuine crooked-tooth smile, and he immediately softened. Yet another reason to avoid orthodontics. For some reason, her smile put people at ease, which was a good thing since her mouth otherwise managed to get her into trouble.

He gave her arm a gentle squeeze. "Nothing to be nervous about. Come with me. We'll locate your friend for the evening."

Friend. The casual way he said it rubbed her the wrong way. A real friend couldn't be bought. Lovers, however, were a different story. Tailor-made for an exposé. Otherwise, she wouldn't be caught dead in a place like this.

Kirby followed Fabian into the main room, where fat white leather-and-chrome Le Corbusier sofas sat empty, except for one in the far, dark corner. A well-dressed woman rested her head on the bare shoulder of a younger, shirtless man, who rubbed her hand as he whispered something to her.

Another man sat alone in one of two black Barcelona chairs, with an ostrich-skin boot propped on the matching ottoman as he sipped wine from an expensive-looking long-stem glass and pressed a cell phone to his ear.

Instrumental lounge versions of pop country singles skimmed the surface of her awareness. It was yet another thread that loosely tied the two establishments together.

Fabian led her out of the main room and into a softly lit hallway lined with closed and semiclosed doors and enclaves with curtains. A black-and-tan patchwork cowhide runner cushioned their footsteps.

As they walked, Kirby reviewed the details of her heartbreaking script. Her persona's husband had been an emotional abuser, a withholder of affection. Her persona hadn't had sex since her engagement. Not even on her wedding night.

If that didn't bring out the so-called friend in a man, nothing would.

She never thought her own life story could be used for something good. Never thought she'd have the nerve to talk about the unspeakable situation she'd found herself in. Being untouched, unloved and disrespected by the person who had stood in front of God and everyone and promised otherwise.

Kirby swallowed back the unscripted tears, along with the shame they carried. This wasn't the time or place to fall apart for real.

"You'll find Ride to be a caring individual. And I can vouch for his integrity," Fabian said as they entered a cozy room at the end of the hallway.

The room didn't have a door. Only an extrawide gas fireplace on the far wall and a solitary tan Le Corbusier sofa facing it. An exit sign midway down the hall had caught her eye as they walked by. She didn't plan on needing to make a quick exit, but the knowledge felt comforting nonetheless.

Fabian did a three-sixty. Confusion twisted the near-perfect features of his gorgeous face. "Ride is usually here. This is his territory."

"You make him sound like some sort of animal."

"I guess that would be a fair description. Make yourself comfortable. I'll find him and let him know you're ready."

Fabian exited the room, leaving her alone. And uneasy. The positioning of the sofa, with its back to the door, made her feel like fresh meat in a lion's den. But this particular assignment required bait, so she sat.

She placed her purse on the near edge of the coffee table, adjusted the camera bauble, then leaned back and waited.

The fireplace felt warm. Too warm. She slipped the elastic band from her wrist and wrangled her long strands into a messy bun on top of her head. It wasn't as if she were trying to impress the guy. For what she was paying, he'd act impressed anyway.

The air-conditioning mercifully kicked on and soothed the back of her neck. In fact, the room started to feel a little too cool.

As she was about to release her hair from the elastic's grip once again, a pair of warm hands slid onto her shoulders, and adept fingers slipped beneath the neck of her cashmere sweater and proceeded to massage her muscles.

Panic comingled with pleasure. The conflicting sensations swirled in her stomach before descending straight to her sex. She never knew a shoulder massage could be so erotic.

The man pressed his lips close to her ear and whispered, "I couldn't find him."

From the corner of her eye, she noticed the rolled-up sleeve of his white unbuttoned shirt.

*Fabian.*

He smelled exceptionally good. Like vanilla and pine. He must have splashed on some aftershave or cologne, just for her. Maybe since her scheduled friend was nowhere to be found, the host felt obligated to step in.

Awesome. She hadn't even met Easy Ride, and he'd already rejected her.

Not that she was complaining. In fact, she might have to reconsider her choice. For now, she'd play along.

"Who were you looking for? Refresh my memory," she said.

"Anyone who can satisfy you the way I can."

Kirby's breath hitched. She hadn't expected that kind of talk. At least, not so soon.

His touch deepened, his thumbs working the knotted muscles of her upper back. She didn't dare move. Still, she had questions. Lots of them.

"How do you know what will satisfy me?" she said nervously. "Maybe I have exotic tastes."

He leaned in again. "Give me an example, and I'll tell you exactly how I could satisfy you. In great detail."

The jagged lump that had settled in her throat dissolved as sweetly and easily as cotton candy. His rich voice alone satisfied her hungry soul. No details required.

With this guy, straight missionary would be enough.

Forget Easy Ride. Fabian was definitely her man tonight. Besides, he was probably the gatekeeper of all the secrets, and would make a great friend. And an even better canary.

But that was secondary. She finally understood what it meant to mix business with pleasure, to live in the moment. *To be touched this way again.* No wonder ladies came here in droves after a heartbreak. When reality ripped a person to shreds, there was no better medicine than a three-dimensional and utterly willing fantasy.

A paid-for fantasy, she reminded herself.

She leaned into the shoulder rub completely, which now included an upper-arm massage.

"I can't get over how good you smell tonight. What kind of perfume are you wearing?" he asked.

Now there was a line if she'd ever heard one. She wasn't wearing perfume. It almost jolted her out of the fantasy. Almost.

"It's called soap and water."

"No, that's not it. It must be *you* that I smell."

A flush of warmth spread through her entire body. He didn't clarify what he meant. She was more than willing to fill in the blanks.

He delved even deeper into her tense shoulder muscles.

"That feels so good," she said, although certain syllables came out as an embarrassing moan.

"And you feel good. Those extra pounds are definitely your friend."

*Huh?*

She tried to peel away from his touch as she struggled to rationalize the backhanded compliment, but he reeled her back in with those amazing hands.

Still, such a comment couldn't go unaddressed. Not for what she was paying.

"Are you insinuating I'm fat?"

"Not at all. But I love the extra meat on your bones. Brings out the animal in me."

Kirby's mind swirled, and not in a good way this time. In fact, it didn't swirl. It shook rather violently.

Even though the guy was sexy as hell, there was definitely something wrong here. As in, mentally.

She was halfway tempted to deliver a strong elbow to the groin and get the hell out of there.

No sooner had the impulsive thought crossed her mind, than the tip of his finger traced an invisible line along the base of her neck and stopped at the most sensitive point on the side, as if marking the spot. He planted the softest, warmest kiss right at the destination, causing an unbearable stimulation. How could he have landed on the exact spot that could launch her straight to the heavens and beyond?

Then he whispered, "Your breasts look especially amazing. If I didn't know better, I'd swear they were natural."

*Seriously?* She leaned forward and reclaimed her back, as well as the backbone that went with it.

"We're done here. Go find my scheduled friend."

There. She'd said it, even though part of her wanted to continue this messed-up game they'd started, if only for more neck kisses and shoulder rubs. Maybe she could pay him to *not* talk.

Kirby stood as best she could on legs that had all but turned to marshmallows.

What little strength she'd managed to compose quickly decomposed when she turned to find an over-the-top-gorgeous brunet stranger staring back at her. His expression could easily be described as horrified. Perhaps as horrified as she felt.

He didn't seem to have a clue as to who she was.

It took a moment, but she sure recognized him. His white shirt was now unbuttoned, and he'd removed his Stetson since rescuing her valet ticket from the dance floor.

His expression remained as distressed as his jeans, yet he looked nothing short of gorgeous. Infuriatingly so, because she didn't want to feel attracted to this nutcase. The image of a black horse, which was inked on his now-exposed chest, seemed to breathe heavily along with him.

"You're not Lydia," he said.

"And you're not Fabian."

He ran both hands through his beautifully disheveled hair, and gripped it down to the roots, as if anchoring himself amid the confusion.

In her opinion, all he did was elevate the bed-head look to a whole new level of sexiness.

"There you are, Ride. I see you two have met," Fabian said, entering the room as if nothing remotely weird had happened in his absence.

For Kirby, the moment had a distinct ménage feel about it. And not in a good way.

As much as Easy Ride had awakened something within her—something completely capable of muddling her emotions—her head began to clear. Obviously, this guy was into some woman named Lydia. Or else he had the ability to cook up some seriously tasty lines that contained no sincere ingredients, and then serve them to everyone. Along with a few borderline-offensive ones specifically for her.

No matter. Kirby smiled, from the inside out. She'd have no problem doing what she needed to do for the story. And maybe doing a few things she wouldn't ordinarily do along the way.

As imperfect as their introduction had been, Easy Ride was perfect story material.

# 2

*HOLY CRAP.*

So this was his new client. From behind, and with her hair up in a bun, she could pass for their manager. Lydia loved his shoulder rubs, neck kisses and harmless-but-naughty banter. The naughtier, the better, with the added levity of some questionable compliments. All in good fun.

Nothing about this current situation could be considered remotely fun.

This Lydia-from-behind look-alike hadn't bantered back in the usual manner, which should have been a clue. Instead, he had ramped up the innuendo.

The fact that this woman wasn't painfully thin should have been another clue, but he'd been too busy enjoying the softness of her to think it through. Rather, enjoying the softness of what he thought was Lydia.

In a way, he was relieved it wasn't his boss because he'd gotten more than a little turned on. Then it struck him. Had he really made a snarky remark about a new client's breasts?

Adam Drake traced the outline of her gorgeous curves

from afar. She'd even let her hair down, and damn if she didn't make the most stunning brunette he'd ever seen.

She'd been a blonde in the club, he was sure of it. No small detail in his defense for what had happened. But the hair color hadn't been the hook. It was her belligerent-turned-appreciative gold-flecked eyes looking directly into his.

Besides, Lydia was the one who'd asked him to track down Gentleman John and report back to her in this room. But she hadn't been here when he'd returned.

Where the hell had Lydia run off to anyway? She could corroborate his story.

Then again, why even bother formulating a defense? Being innocent never worked. At least, not for him.

He tried to remain confident as the client chatted with Fabian near the door, probably requesting a new friend for the evening. All the while, his good buddy Fab acted proper and professional and appropriately appalled at Adam's behavior.

Now *that* was hilarious. Fab put on a bigger act than all the guys combined.

Fabian finally gave him the two-fingered wave, indicating it was safe to come back. He would probably be asked to apologize to the classy client. And Fabian would soak it all up and use it against him later.

Instead of a reprimand, Fabian said, "She's happy to continue with you."

"Come again?" Adam said.

An amused smile slashed across his client's face. She didn't seem too torn up, which made him wonder whether she had some sort of ulterior motive. She sure as hell didn't look as if she had to pay some poor schmuck to hear her out. Much less praise her.

If he were good at one thing, it was spotting a poseur. A woman who came in for all the wrong reasons. Namely, for sex with one of the hot guys. Clients didn't have to pay a penny if they weren't satisfied with their session. That much was in the contract. So if a client wanted sex, the employee risked losing his wages if he said no.

Fabian left without responding to Adam's question, but the knowing wink spoke volumes. He'd saved Adam's ass on this one, as a best friend should.

He also left Adam to comfort this heartbroken knockout.

Fabian was the only other person who knew Adam's own story of heartbreak. How his fiancée had traded up to the lead singer of the popular country-rock band Better Days. But only after cheating behind his back for an embarrassing amount of time.

He fought the urge to rub his bicep. The tattoo artist had inked a gorgeous stallion over his ex-girlfriend's name. It was a nice complement to the Arabian mare tattooed on his chest. The cursive letters of Liv's name had transformed into the stallion's windblown mane quite easily. But he could still feel the resulting humiliation at times. Like slivers of glass lodged under his skin.

After a few awkward moments of silence, Adam offered his hand and led his new client back to the sofa.

She settled in on the far side.

He closed the distance between them, then draped his arm across the back. Near her, but not touching. He owed her that much.

"So, how does this work?" she asked, then bit her luscious bottom lip, which took a close second in sensuality to the top one. Full, with a cupid's bow.

He resisted the urge to bite his own bottom lip.

"No rules. It can work however you want. It's helpful for me to know a little bit about you. Why you're here."

"I heard about this place from my best friend, who will remain unnamed."

"Understood."

She fidgeted with her hands for several seconds while he waited. Patiently. He tried like hell not to get a full hard-on just looking at her. He felt the stirrings of one, a slight tightening of his jeans, so he diverted his gaze back to the fireplace.

"I'm divorced," she said. "Which was difficult enough. But I was never really married. Not in the way people are usually married. Oh, God, this is hard."

He tried to follow, but she wasn't making sense.

"Were you in some sort of arranged marriage?"

She responded with a nervous laugh and shook her head.

"No. Nothing like that."

He slid somewhat closer. Close enough to pull her in. If, and only if, she wanted.

Soap and water, did she say? Whatever it was, she smelled damn good. Thinking of the way her soft skin had felt against his palms made the blood rush to his hands, as well as to other extremities.

"You don't have to say anything if you don't want. But, if you do, I'm obligated to keep your secret. I signed a confidentiality agreement. Nothing leaves this room," he said.

The disclaimer earned him a direct look. One he couldn't quite decipher.

Perhaps he couldn't read her thoughts, but he could definitely read the heartbreak in her eyes.

He swallowed hard and proceeded to bend his personal rule. The one about not making the first move. But hadn't he already smashed it to pieces?

*Again, not my fault...*

He urged her gently toward him, and she followed his lead. Her head rested on his shoulder as he caressed her arm, which he knew to be softer than the cashmere sweater that covered it.

Before his thoughts could stray any further, he reminded himself of his role. A shoulder to cry on. Nothing more.


KIRBY COULDN'T FORCE out the words even though she had rehearsed them to death.

Thankfully, he didn't push.

Although her true story might eventually encourage him to open up, she couldn't bring herself to do it, even though part of her needed to tell someone, anyone, so badly.

She totally got the concept behind The Deep now. Understood the service these men provided. Maybe if she'd come to a place like this after her own heartbreak, she'd be healed.

Rather than keep talking, Kirby yearned for this stranger to kiss the back of her neck again. Was it okay to ask for that?

Yet, she didn't want to ask for any physical affection. She'd been rejected after asking in the past, and she would never make that mistake again.

No, she wanted and needed this man to make the first move. Paid for or otherwise.

As if he sensed her need to be touched, he brushed an errant strand of hair from her face.

Her eyes went directly to his sensual mouth, which promised so much pleasure without uttering a word.

She wanted to know how it would feel to kiss him. She needed to kiss this stranger, she decided, seconds before he leaned in and pressed that gorgeous mouth softly against hers.

A sudden wave of self-consciousness prompted Kirby to pull away, even though she would have liked nothing more than for him to nudge her lips apart. Open a simple part of herself she'd effectively sealed off.

"Sorry. I shouldn't have initiated that," he said.

"Club policy?"

"My policy."

Obviously, his personal policy wasn't the least bit compatible with hers. The only option now was to save face.

"It's okay. Paid-for kisses aren't exactly what I need."

He seemed to contemplate her admission.

"Then I'll stop the clock, kiss you for ten minutes, then we'll resume with the paid-for session. How does that sound?"

All of a sudden she was hyperaware of their proximity, how utterly strong and protective his arm felt around her, how his sensual mouth would feel while exploring her own, if she wanted it.

And she definitely wanted.

"Why would you do that?" she asked.

"I want to kiss you. Why else?"

Before she could overanalyze it, he pressed his mouth against hers and tenderly nudged her lips apart with his tongue.

She granted him full access, and he explored deeper.

He tasted mostly of mint and slightly of Scotch. She wanted to consume him, as he had begun to consume her.

For the next several minutes, her feelings swung from

one end of the emotional spectrum to the other. From being convinced that he enjoyed the deep and intimate kisses as much as she did, to wondering whether this was nothing more than a job duty, then back to being convinced.

As Kirby struggled to stop the pendulum on *convinced*, someone cleared his throat behind them. It was enough to jolt some sense into apparently both of them, as they broke away from the kiss at the same time and turned to look.

*Fabian.*

Easy Ride shook his head and flashed the fingers of one hand. Twice. Indicating ten more minutes of privacy, she assumed. He turned back to her.

Once again, she had his baby blues' full attention. Had she really been making out with this unbelievably sexy man? One who'd made the first move, and was giving his affection at no charge?

Maybe these guys operated like crack dealers. Give the customer a free taste and get 'em hooked. Maybe she definitely needed what he was offering.

"You're really not charging me for the kissing time? I thought you were joking."

"I wouldn't joke about something like that." He leaned in to kiss her again, resuming the tender urgency they'd generated before the interruption.

As if Kirby was no longer in control of her own body, she leaned back and guided him to more of a full-frontal connection.

He accepted her lead. In fact, they seemed to have the same idea as they repositioned themselves on the sofa. Her underneath. Him on top. By the time he pressed into her, he was rock-hard.

Her private gratefulness momentarily took her breath away.

Pure desire took over from there as he nudged her thighs apart and situated himself between them while continuing to kiss her. The friction against the inseam of her jeans rubbed her in the most delicious way, and with exactly the right amount of tension.

All the while, an instrumental lounge version of George Strait's "Baby Blue" serenaded the edge of her consciousness.

The slow, confident movement of his hips combined with the softness of his mouth had her mind so twisted and stirred and shaken that she barely noticed his hands reaching underneath and cupping her behind.

He moved her hips for her, pulling her into his deeper thrusts with a slow, smooth, effortless rhythm. The angle and intensity took her all the way.

The pent-up tension and the subsequent release in full were almost more than she could handle, yet she somehow managed to hold in the heaviest groan. It had been so long. So long since she'd wanted a man and felt this wanted in return.

With the final deep thrust against her, he softly moaned, "Oh, baby."

Her mind began to clear as he finished. Unfortunately, her clear mind always invited the most unwanted of thoughts. Now, her thoughts insisted this gorgeous man would ultimately reject her, as her ex-husband had done, even though she wasn't here for personal reasons. Or, at least, she wasn't supposed to be.

Combine business and pleasure? Live in the moment? Those luxuries were for other people. Her choices had always been entwined with consequences.

Consequences. So many of them in this particular situation.

*What have I done?*

*WHAT THE HELL am I doing?*

That was the first thought to cross Adam's mind, once the blood rushed back to his brain. It was as if he had no self-control around this one. As in, zero.

One thing was for sure, he couldn't accept her money. Any of it. Hopefully, she wouldn't insist he take it. If she did, her intentions would be clear.

Awkward. The whole damn thing was awkward.

After they both eased back to the upright position, he put his arm around her shoulder and kissed her on top of her gloriously mussed-up hair. If he wasn't mistaken, she sharply inhaled, as if the casual familiarity were somehow inappropriate.

"Next time, I won't initiate," he said, hoping to drive home that his intention had not been to ravage her. "You're just so fucking gorgeous, I couldn't hold back."

Her reluctance softened, and she embraced him in return.

"It felt good. I mean, *really* good," she said. "Thank you."

He relinquished his embrace when she stretched forward to retrieve her purse.

"Did I call you *baby*?" he asked, because in the heat of it all, he couldn't be sure.

"Yeah. You did."

"Sorry. In my defense, I don't know your name. Somehow 181 didn't feel right."

Her hand welcomed his as they stood and walked to the exit, which was a relief. Some of the women simply charged out the door with a satisfied grin.

The other guys were more than okay with that outcome. Even though Adam still felt bitter as hell about what had happened with Liv, he never liked to end an intimate encounter in such a crass way. Not even when it merely imitated the real thing.

Once outside, he pulled her a little closer, creating as private a goodbye as he could. After all, this might be the last time he ever saw her.

"I'm glad you were satisfied with the service. Be sure to fill out the online customer satisfaction survey at your earliest convenience." Might as well add some levity to the situation. The worst thing that could happen would be his humor falling flat.

"I thought you kissed me, and everything else, because you wanted to. But I'll give you high marks on the survey anyway."

He gulped. Hard. Part of him wanted that type of response. The other part didn't want the confusion of it. But he needed it, and it felt damn good to admit it. If only to himself.

Did he have the right to ask her to come back? Or, better yet, go on a proper date?

A chuckle rose in his throat at the absurdity of it. Why the hell would she want to go out with a guy who worked here? Who—she must have thought—does this sort of thing with other women? And for money.

She must have picked up on his thoughts because she backed away.

"I need to get home," she said, her eyes diverting from his in favor of the valet, who had pulled her car around.

"Call me if you encounter any problems along the way. Flat tire, that sort of thing."

It was an impulsive and potentially brilliant demand.

And entirely true. Even though women could take care of themselves, he hated the idea of her out alone at night.

"I don't have your number," she said.

Adam sprinted to the valet to borrow a pen, then sprinted back. He turned her hand over and jotted his cell number into her palm.

"So you change flat tires?" she asked.

"One of my little-known talents."

"Perhaps you should have a business card. Something like 'mends flat tires and broken hearts.'"

A sense of humor, too. That made her a triple threat. Gorgeous, smart and funny.

As she drove away, he had the most selfish thought imaginable.

*Please, let her get a flat.*


"Should I call HAZMAT?" Fabian asked.

Had the guy really been standing by the back door the entire time?

"Very funny, Fab. Issue her a refund."

Adam sidestepped his supposed best friend and walked back inside, toward the den of iniquity.

The refund request implied an admission, but no way he'd take her money. Sure, they hadn't broken the cardinal rule. But he'd initiated something and violated his own rule in the process.

How did the other guys live with themselves, letting their clients pay for their sessions after the line was crossed? Collecting their fat commission for what could barely be considered work? And when they care nothing about these women?

*They do perfectly fine.* More than fine, actually. They drove Porsches, rather than a beat-up Jeep.

He'd been one bad decision away from buying a

Porsche himself, until the false accusation from a client at his former job convinced him not to blow what little savings he had. The worst part of it wasn't the car. It was how his boss didn't believe his side of the story, even after their years of friendship and mutual professional respect.

"Asshole," he muttered under his breath just as he bumped shoulders with one of the other guys.

"Who are you callin' an asshole, Ride? Watch where you're goin'."

"Sorry, man. I was talking to myself."

"Sounds boring," the guy countered.

*Asshole.*

Once in the men's room, he splashed cold water on his face. He hadn't lost this kind of control, fully clothed, with a woman since he was sixteen.

He yanked a paper towel from the dispenser and patted his skin dry. Didn't even hear anyone come in.

"Please tell me you used protection," Fabian said as he proceeded to toss some half-full glasses of red wine down the sink.

"Of course. Wouldn't want my client to catch any of my multiple STDs, would I?"

"Or for you to catch one."

Adam struggled to not rise to her defense, even though the two of them hadn't ventured anywhere near such a delicate topic.

"Can we change the subject, please? Do I have anyone else on the books tonight? I'd like to get out of here," Adam said.

"Nope."

"How about tomorrow night?"

"Last time I checked you were booked solid. Good

thing you asked for Saturday off. You're going to need the rest."

"Is she on the books?"

"She? You mean 181? Nope."

"'Nope'? You are an exceptional linguist."

"And a cunning one, too. At least, that's what the ladies tell me. It's all in the tongue."

With a half smile, Adam said, "I'll take your word for it. Now, give it up, Fab."

Fabian kept his head down. Kept busy swirling soap and water around in the glasses and dodging the demand in the process.

"Well?" Adam asked.

"I don't know what you mean."

"Her name."

"That's confidential. I could lose my job. But I do have a question."

"You have a question, but you won't answer mine? Asshole."

Fabian made a show of clearing his throat and said, "Ever been to the Armadillo Palace?"

"You already know the answer. We've been there together."

"What street is it on? I can't remember."

"Kirby."

Fabian smiled. "Yes. You are correct."

*Kirby.* Adam had to smile, as well.

He grabbed his cell from the counter and the thing practically vibrated right out of his hand. His heartbeat kicked up a notch or three at the possibility it was her.

Although the area code was in Houston, the number wasn't familiar.

He stepped into the hallway.

"Adam here." Not that Kirby would know his first name, but he wouldn't mind if she did.

"Hey, Adam. It's Bernard."

Adam's chest constricted at the sound of his attorney's voice.

"Why do I have a feeling this is bad news," he said.

"It isn't the worst news, but I didn't want to wait until morning."

"Burning the midnight oil at home? How much is that going to cost me?"

"I told you not to worry about costs. I'll draw my compensation from the countersuit we win."

"Oh, yeah? Whom am I suing, and for what?"

"Defamation. Now, don't get upset, but I saw a rather damning statement your ex-boss recently made, in print, about you."

Flames of rage shot up Adam's spine at the prospect.

"Is that a fact? What does it say?"

"He claims some Hermès saddles went missing around the time you were dismissed. Looks like he's setting the stage for something."

# 3

KIRBY RESTED HER head on her desk for a measly ten seconds before a hard double-knock jolted her from her borderline-REM state. She didn't have to look up to know it was Seth Wainright.

"No, I didn't get the story. Yet," she called out from her slump. Against her better judgment, she looked up anyway.

Seth leaned in, and for a moment she was afraid he'd wobble over and crush her.

"Too bad. I was looking forward to the video. But, hey, we don't all get lucky the first time," he said. The words were ushered out by the fumes of coffee and onions.

She sat up straight, and not only to find some fresh air.

*The video.* She'd stayed up late, watching the dark, grainy footage over and over again. The only thing she'd noticed was how she'd totally lost control. They both had. The video couldn't be used as evidence against the club, but it reminded her of how good it felt to experience such intimacy. In any case, she had no intention of sharing the footage with anyone. Especially not Seth.

"I'm going back in tonight," she said without embellishment.

It wasn't a complete lie. She hadn't booked anything. But her neck ached to be massaged, her body hurt to be held, her mouth burned to be kissed. It was as if she'd caught the flu, and the best medicine would only make matters worse.

Seth lingered. And he wasn't the lingering type.

"What's it like in there?" he asked.

"Surprisingly classy. Gorgeous, partially undressed men."

"Private rooms?"

"Lots of rooms, but I wasn't in a private one."

"Book one. Tonight. Force a confession. Or, in this case, seduce one out of him. That's what I'd do," he whispered, then wobbled away.

Although she couldn't visualize anyone being seduced by Seth, he was right about one thing. Time to put on her big-girl panties. *Just be ready and willing to take them off, according to Seth.*

Not that the station condoned "going all the way" to get the story, but they didn't outright discourage it, either.

Kirby logged in to the private portal. Unfortunately, Easy Ride was booked tonight. No slots available tomorrow night, either. Which meant he'd be with other women, likely doing to them what he'd done to her.

The thought slammed into her unexpectedly. No way should she be jealous. Yet, she couldn't stop thinking about how a total stranger could feel so good and so right. Even if it was only so "right now."

The phone rang, yanking her out of her messed-up thoughts.

"Montgomery here," she answered.

"I got a lead on a stray Dumpster diver near Hobby Airport. Can you help?"

"Good morning, Reese. Of course I'll help, but calling me with this information is only going to distract me from work until I can get away."

"All part of my evil plan. Can you get away now?"

Kirby weighed the situation. In times like these, she wished she was unemployed and independently wealthy, like her best friend, Reese, and could scour the city for animals in need of rescuing. Talk about the ultimate dream job.

"I might be able to arrange something. Have you already lined up a foster?" Kirby asked.

"No. But don't worry. I'll foster until I can find someone."

Kirby exhaled a breath she hadn't realized she was holding. The easy part was catching an animal. The harder part was placing him or her in a loving home. And the absolute worst part was saying goodbye, once a home was found. That was how she'd recently ended up with a rescue cat. At her house, foster home had turned into forever home.

"How far away?

"South of Broadway, living behind the Dumpsters at some rather seedy apartments. I tried to execute a solo rescue earlier this morning, but I couldn't get close."

"No chance the owner lives in the complex?"

"If that's the case, the puppy needs rescuing more than ever. Very thin and dirty."

"I'll take an early lunch. Pick me up at ten thirty," Kirby said. She wasn't going to get any further on The Deep story this afternoon. Might as well be distracted for a worthy cause.

"Great. I'll wait up front."

Kirby replaced the receiver and referred back to the website. As she clicked through the photos, someone approached from behind.

She recognized the fumes.

"Which one is yours?" Seth asked. "Please tell me it's Gentleman John. Ha! Gotta love it."

Seth launched into his obnoxious laugh, which always had a delayed effect. Like a time bomb with a long fuse.

Today, it was more like a stink bomb.

As soon as Kirby clicked on Easy Ride and his buff upper body filled the screen, the laughing ceased.

Seth leaned in closer.

Kirby held her breath.

"What's his name?" he asked.

"They don't give out names."

"Find out. Or I will."

Strange. Something had piqued his curiosity, and it likely wasn't Easy Ride's abundance of chiseled muscles.

"You seem awfully interested. Why?" she asked.

"Only trying to help. In fact, the offer still stands to trade stories. The oil-and-gas lead is a sure thing. I'd hate to see you blow your only chance with Bettencourt after you waited so long."

Even though she doubted Seth's concern for her professional well-being, he wasn't simply blowing smoke. Their news director had earned the nickname "one-chance Charlie" for good reason. He gave reporter wannabes who worked at the station a shot to be on the air. A single shot. This was hers.

"Why are *you* so interested in The Deep?" Seth asked. "Aside from getting to hang out at the beefcake buffet. A story like this will cast your reputation in stone. Good-bye, good girl."

"Oddly enough, you just answered your own question."

Seth raised one bushy brow and gave her a nod of approval. He only related to people who got down in the mud. No doubt her willingness to chase this particular lead earned his reluctant respect.

What she didn't tell him was that this story had become personal long before she'd stepped foot in The Deep. The thought of men taking women's money for false flattery reminded her too much of her charming crook of an ex-husband, who was more than happy to relieve her of any and all loose change and limited savings, only to end up spending it on his girlfriends. Oh, and then going on to reject his own wife.

She mentally returned to the sofa at The Deep. No evidence of rejection there. No usable information, either. He didn't even charge her for the kisses.

Certain facts about the club might be difficult to get out of Easy Ride. However, the pleasure promised to be deliciously...easy. So much so, she was finding it hard to focus today.

*Goodbye, good girl was right.*

"HEY, FAB. SPOT ME," Adam said.

Fabian positioned himself, ready to catch the bar in case Adam's ambitious 320-pound bench press turned out to be a top-story bleeder on the evening news.

"You trying to kill yourself, Ride?"

Adam grimaced at the weight, but damn if Better Days's newest release wasn't blaring from every speaker throughout the gym. The angry schmuck within him could bench-press an eighteen-wheeler to the lead singer's whiny voice. The owner of Six-Pax usually had better taste in music.

He finished a set and Fabian helped with the bar.

"No death wish, but that song makes me want to kill someone."

Fabian slapped Adam on the back with the appropriate force. The gesture implied friendly support rather than pity.

"Sorry, man. How anyone can work out to that country-rock shit is beyond me. I'll tell the manager to change the station."

"Don't bother. I might as well get used to hearing it. Better Days is having its best days."

"I thought you were over her," Fabian said.

Adam considered Fab's statement for a minute. Truth was, being dumped by Liv honestly didn't hurt anymore. He couldn't say the same for the humiliation.

"I wish her the best of luck. She'll need it. Her new boyfriend has quite the reputation with groupies. I imagine karma will take care of the balance due."

Adam wandered over to the free weights next. Fabian trailed close behind.

"I still can't wrap my mind around how she was doing him at the same time she was doing you. And for so long," Fabian said.

So much for friendly support.

"Gee, Fab, let's see if the other guys want to sit in on this discussion. I think one of them might not have caught the last part."

Not that it mattered. Everyone within an earshot already knew the scoop.

Adam grabbed a pair of forty pounders and started banging out some standing curls.

Fabian followed suit, but grabbed some thirties instead. "I bet I know how to cheer you up."

"How so?"

"Your new girlfriend, Kirby, tried to book tonight. Saw it on the activity feed."

Adam nearly dropped the weights. It felt as if someone had tickled his goddamn heart with a feather.

"Why do you think I'd be happy?"

"For starters, you've never humped a first-timer then played the concerned-boyfriend card."

"I've never humped a client. Period. I shouldn't even have to say it."

"First time for everything, my friend. If you didn't hump her, why did you ask me to refund her money?"

"I like her. She's attractive. We made out and I enjoyed the hell out of it. What can I say?"

"Just don't do what the others are doing. Eventually, one of these wounded lovelies is going to turn psycho and give us away, and then we'll be in some deep shit."

Adam continued doing reps. All he could think was how he'd love to break a rule or two with Kirby. But it sure as hell wasn't going to happen at the club.

"Does Lydia know?" Adam asked.

"I suspect our madam chooses not to know. But have no fear. Even if we get busted, you're clean. Or so you say."

Although true, it did nothing to tame the uneasy feeling. Last thing he needed was another controversy. Not if he wanted to land the gig in Florida. They needed an elite trainer. He needed a new life. Seemed like the perfect fit. It had been a year since he'd been appreciated for what he did best: train riders and horses at the most prestigious grounds in the greater Houston Area.

Wild Indigo Equestrian Center seemed to be the only potential employer left in the world who either didn't know about his previous legal problems, or didn't care. They certainly didn't need to know his current employment situation, or the newest dilemma with the saddles. Either one of those would knock him out of the running.

He grabbed his gym bag from the floor, shrugged off his sweaty T-shirt and donned a fresh one. Six hours before he had to be back at work. Enough time to make a dent in the informal written deposition he'd promised Bernard.

The real question was, why would his ex-boss levy those charges so long after Adam had left? Why would it even be a case, because there was no way the man could have proof? Proof didn't exist. None of it made sense.

Adam pulled his cell phone from his bag. One voice message, and from a number he didn't recognize. Maybe it was Kirby. Maybe she got a flat tire after all.

He held the phone to his ear, and as far away from Fabian as possible.

"This is Methodist Hospital. We're trying to locate Adam Drake, next of kin for Henry Drake. Please give us a call at…"

The hot ringing in his head made it impossible to hear the number.

Next of kin? Isn't that the kind of thing people said when someone was deceased, or on their death bed? Besides, Adam was the man's only kin.

A sudden sheen of cold sweat traversed the length of his neck and back. He swallowed hard in an attempt to jump-start his breathing. Instead of calling the hospital, he sprinted out of Six-Pax, jumped into his Jeep without bothering to buckle the seat belt and tore out of the parking lot.

He had zero intention of driving the speed limit. Didn't care how many tickets he got along the way.

Time to start breaking some rules.

KIRBY POSITIONED HERSELF on one side of the Dumpster while Reese tiptoed around to the other.

The air reeked of urine and spoiled milk and miscellaneous unidentifiable odors. She inhaled through her mouth, but pure nastiness coated her throat. The thick, noxious mix made her feel as if she were swallowing toxic sludge. But it was all worth it as soon as the scared puppy peeked around the side. In fact, there was no other place Kirby would rather be.

Except perhaps one other place. On the sofa at The Deep, being massaged and kissed and desired by the most desirable man she'd ever met. And being looked at by those baby blue eyes.

The memory battled for her focus, but dreamy eyes of a different kind were sizing her up.

"Looks like a Maltese-terrier mix," she said.

The puppy growled as if in disagreement.

"Hard to tell. Baby needs a bath. At least his vocal cords are healthy," Reese said.

They anchored the edges of a large net at either corner of a fence without managing to spook the puppy, and draped the rest of it over the large metal contraption.

"Area secure," Kirby said, although she knew all too well the puppy could finagle its way out of the trap easily enough.

Kirby pulled the net over her head, effectively sealing her inside the entrapment zone. She opened the paper sack, reached in and tore off a piece of the hamburger and bun. Then she held it out while Reese snuck underneath from the other side, rescue leash in hand.

The puppy crouched and took a few tentative steps forward, but retracted back to its spot without taking the bait.

Kirby set down the bite and backed away as far as the net would allow.

Reese took slow, easy steps closer. Then they both stood perfectly still. And waited.

It took a few minutes, but the puppy inched close enough to claim the food, then scurried back to the unreachable center behind the Dumpster.

"Smart little guy. Or girl," Reese said.

"My bets are on girl. Time to take it to the next level." Kirby placed another bite even farther outside the puppy's self-defined boundary.

The creature gained a little more confidence, grabbing the bite this time and retreating before Reese could make her move.

"Party time," Kirby whispered.

Reese moved to the edge of the Dumpster. The puppy would surely see her feet, but would hopefully forget all about it once the feast was laid out.

Kirby set two pieces of the burger on the ground, a couple of feet apart, along with a trail of French fries leading up to her feet as she backed completely against the netting. If the puppy wanted to claim all treats, he or she would inevitably linger.

Sure enough, the puppy took the bait.

Reese slipped the leash around the puppy's neck while Kirby peeled away the netting.

The puppy railed against the leash but then seemed to finally realize they were there to help and relinquished its struggle on the way to the car.

Once settled in the backseat, the creature proceeded to lick Kirby's face.

"Ah, more kisses." She tore off a tiny bite of the burger as a reward.

"Boy or girl?" Reese asked as she started the car and took the first U-turn toward downtown.

Kirby lifted the little one's wagging tail.

"Girl. I win."

"You're amazing. How did you know?"

"Easy. A boy would have taken the bait on the first drop and thought about the consequences later."

Reese raised a brow and glanced in the rearview mirror. "Are we talking about dogs or men?"

Kirby simply smiled.

"Thank you for doing this. I know you're really busy at work," Reese said.

"Happy to do it."

The puppy curled up beside Kirby and fell fast asleep as they rode, in relative silence, back to the station.

"Speaking of work and kisses, how did your date go last night?" Reese asked.

Kirby figured the question had been percolating in her friend's brain.

"Okay. He's amazing-looking, but otherwise I have no story to tell." She privately smiled at her understatement, and Reese totally witnessed the momentary slip.

"Keep your eyes on the road, please," Kirby admonished. "We don't want to kill the puppy after we went to so much trouble to rescue her."

"Okay. But dish, please."

"There's nothing to dish. Seriously, I'm not planning on sleeping with the guy. I just need to get him to talk."

"Right. No telling where those guys have been."

"Probably no more places than my ex had been," Kirby said.

"Oh. Sorry, I forgot. Hey, know what? I think you should totally go for it with this guy. Get the story, and have a few orgasms."

"What? No." But even as Kirby said it, her body begged to differ.

"Do it, Kirby. You deserve to have some fun. Just make him wear protection."

Reese eased to a stop in front of the station.

"I won't let it go that far," Kirby said as she exited the backseat, much to the disappointment of the puppy.

Reese's smirk said it all. Kirby hadn't been the least bit convincing.

Maybe because she didn't feel the least bit convinced. Mostly, what she felt was a deep stirring that whipped into a frenzy at the thought of him. It was as if he'd turned her on last night and there wasn't an off switch.

Between the high of rescuing the puppy and the images of Easy Ride that her mind feasted on, getting anything accomplished at work wouldn't be easy.

Once back at her desk, a different reality set in. She hadn't logged out of the private portal, and someone had obviously been poking around the site. Furthermore, she knew exactly who that someone was. But there was no way she'd let Seth hijack her assignment.

True, she had a chink in her armor, which could make it more challenging to be objective. Yet, she wanted to feel what this man had made her feel. She deserved to feel something. All the self-talk in the world kept leading her back to the same place, and back into the arms of the irresistible unknown.

*Mix business with pleasure...live in the moment.*

The only problem was, she hadn't been prepared for... *this*. Out-of-control desire. As appealing as it sounded to shed her good-girl image, she hadn't set out to sleep with her source. Too risky. Professionally and personally.

In fact, she'd be satisfied with a repeat of last night's "performance."

*Yeah. Right.*

At least she was prepared to take Reese's advice, should the uncontrollable happen again—make him wear a condom—because she was in too deep to stop now. For the pleasure, and for the story.

Her moment, it seemed, had arrived.

ADAM PUMPED A generous amount of Purell into his hands and worked it through every pore. The cool gel calmed his sweaty palms, and the clean scent cleared his head for what he was about to face.

He was still reeling from the emotional jolt, as if he'd been riding the most incredible mare and was cold-cocked by a low-hanging branch.

It didn't help his nervousness to see the name *Henry V. Drake* on the wall next to his grandfather's hospital room.

At least his worst fears weren't realized. Henry hadn't died. From what little Adam had been told when he'd asked for directions at the nurses' station, his grandfather took the wrong dosage of one of his many medicines and blacked out on the front lawn. Fortunately, a neighbor called 911 and gave Adam as the primary contact.

He knocked lightly while easing the door fully open.

"Come in, come in!" Henry's cheery greeting provided some assurance that nothing essential had changed.

The man looked up as Adam approached. A rather large glob of pudding wobbled on the spoon as Henry's hand shook ever so slightly.

"What the heck are you doing here, son? The hospital folks weren't supposed to bother you with this." Henry set down the spoon and shoved the entire tray aside.

Adam perched on the edge of the bed.

"You gave everyone quite a scare, old man."

"Busybody neighbors. I was resting on the lawn. I wish they'd mind their own business."

As if to emphasize his point, Henry kicked at the covers, exposing one pale thin leg and one foot sheathed in a fuzzy blue sock, complete with rubber speed bumps on the sole.

"You were resting, facedown, on the lawn?"

"Okay. Maybe I got a little dizzy."

"You and I are going to put together a written schedule for your medications. Or, better yet, hire a nurse to stop by the house and administer them. I promise I'll find a pretty one."

A little life returned to Henry's pale cheeks.

"I'd rather you find a pretty one for yourself. Nurse or otherwise."

"I'm working on it." Adam couldn't help but smile when he thought about Kirby, which was absolutely insane. But she was insanely beautiful. And seemingly sweet. She sure as hell smelled sweet, and tasted even sweeter.

Henry eyed him curiously. "You've met someone."

"I'm paging the doctor. You're delusional."

"I raised you. I know when you've got a crush."

Crush? It hadn't even occurred to Adam to describe it that way.

As much as he'd like to get to know Kirby better, his plans didn't include a relationship. In fact, that was the last complication he needed, now that his professional life was inching closer to full resurrection. But, hey, his grandfather was happy. Might as well use it to his advantage.

"Okay. You got me. I'll spill the details after you're back home. And only if you let me hire a nurse."

Henry kicked off the remainder of the covers, exposing both legs and damn near everything remotely attached.

Adam arranged Henry's gown to fully cover the man's privates.

"They're keeping me overnight. They want to run some more blasted tests. You'll have to at least feed me a crumb."

A nurse walked in. The doctor followed on her heels.

"What's the verdict?" Adam asked.

"Terrible news. I'm afraid I can't let you run the Houston Marathon this year, Mr. Drake," the doctor said, directing his answer to Henry.

"Well, that is disappointing. I was so sure it was mine to win."

"I don't doubt it for a minute." The doctor turned his attention to Adam. "It could have been much worse. He could have fallen on cement, rather than grass."

"Hey! I'm in the room! I can hear you," Henry interjected. Obviously, he wasn't thrilled about being referred to in the third person. "I was taking a nap. Why doesn't anyone believe me?"

"Do you think he'll be released tomorrow?" Adam asked.

"We'll have to see." The doctor reached down and patted Henry's arm. "I'll give your grandson a call if anything changes."

"I'll spend the night here," Adam said.

The doctor nodded and left the room.

"You're going home, and that's that. There's something I need you to do," Henry said.

"I know. But I don't think we should list our homes until I get a solid offer. It's between me and one other guy, but they pretty much guaranteed I'm in the lead."

"Oh, I'm not worried about that. Destin, Florida, is our destiny! I've already cut the tags off my new swimming trunks, that's how confident I am. Do whatever you think is best as far as putting the houses up for sale."

Adam studied this frail man, who also happened to be the strongest person he knew. A man who spent what should have been his golden years of retirement raising Adam in Houston, putting up with an endless amount of bullshit. Florida was Adam's chance to make it up to the man who had sacrificed so much. Didn't get much better than white sand beaches and emerald-tinted waters.

"So, what is it you need me to do?" Adam asked.

"I want you to promise you'll make me a great-grandfather before I die. I always wanted the word *great* in front of my name."

"How do you know you don't already have great-grandkids running around somewhere?"

Even joking about such a thing made Adam's conscience quiver. Condoms were nonnegotiable until a committed relationship was established. He could be certain of his fatherhood status, or lack thereof, at this point.

"At least promise me you'll find a nice girl. Liv wasn't nice. I may not be much, but I'm a flawless judge of character."

Yet, if Henry really knew what Adam had made of himself—disgraced trainer turned cut-rate escort—it might turn the man's whole flawless-judge assumption on its ear. Considering he could lose his grandfather at any time, it was more important than ever that he straighten out his own life.

Beginning with his career.

# 4

KIRBY STAYED IN bed and stared at her open palm, willing her mind to reconstruct the smudge of what used to be Easy Ride's cell phone number. It had survived the first night and one full day, but last night's bubble bath proved to be its undoing.

She'd committed the sequence to memory, but now the order of the numbers proved to be a moving target. A mental shell game.

When she couldn't find any definition within the hopeless blur, she balled her hand into a fist and knocked herself on the forehead. Hard.

Maybe it was a good thing she didn't write his number down somewhere. She didn't need to become addicted to a man like him. Which meant she'd need to check her emotions and insecurities at the door, along with her newly reawakened carnal desire.

Once halfheartedly upright, she finagled out from under the goose-down comforter, swung her legs over the side of the bed and eased into her fuzzy leopard-print slippers. Onward to the kitchen, where the Keurig sat ready and waiting for its morning abuse.

Designer caffeine. Yet another addiction she couldn't afford. Today could easily be a four-mug day.

She sensed Lady's inquisitive green feline eyes watching her every move from the top of the refrigerator. Kirby retrieved a tin of moist cat food from the pantry. Lady's warm purr couldn't compete with a modified version of the song playing in Kirby's head.

*Baby Blue...*

She wished she could get another look at those blue eyes this morning. Blue skies were out there, as well, but she couldn't see them, either. Nothing but overcast skies.

What her loft lacked in square footage, it more than made up for in windows. Mainly, windows that overlooked a covered parking garage, the adjacent office building and the street directly below.

If only her windows opened, she wouldn't feel so claustrophobic.

Open windows would help in other ways. The smell of shrimp in aspic this early in the morning triggered Kirby's gag reflex. Peeling back the lid of the cat food was like unzipping a body bag containing a swamp-logged corpse. But Lady was worth the inevitable assault on the senses.

She set the plate on the floor and reached into the cabinet for the box of much-needed caffeine. "My turn now."

Or not. The K-cups box was empty.

*Crap.* She'd meant to stop by the grocery store last night, but her thoughts had been consumed by something else entirely.

A caffeine deficit constituted an emergency, so she trudged the mercifully short distance to the bathroom as best she could unfueled.

She pulled her hair back into a slick ponytail, brushed her teeth and washed her face, then slipped out of her satin pajamas and into some black yoga pants and an oversized burnt-orange University of Texas jersey. Good enough for grocery shopping, especially at this early hour. The only people tooling around were…

*Oh, my God.* She *had* seen Fabian before. At one of the nearby grocery stores, although not the one she usually frequented. Who could miss the hottie in his workout attire? He always seemed too consumed with his task to realize most of the women there were ogling him. Herself included.

Chances were slim that he'd be there this morning, but it couldn't hurt to try. Running into him outside the club might make him more comfortable to eventually open up.

"I'll be right back," she explained to Lady as she rushed around in search of her purse and keys.

Sure, the kitty wouldn't understand the words, but she wanted to communicate as sweetly as possible to this particular rescue animal because she knew Lady's history. Why people tortured black cats on Halloween was unimaginable. That's why she'd decided to officially adopt her.

Two abused souls helping each other heal, Kirby concluded.

Another creature possessed the power to make her forget why she'd ever been sad. Fabian had been right. Easy Ride was an animal. Lion-strong and equally undomesticated, yet so enticing to touch. The mere thought of his warm hands, tender, hot mouth and scorching hardness made every inch of her flesh ache.

As soon as Lady finished licking the remainder of aspic from her plate, Kirby scooped her up for an official good-morning hug and retrieved her cell phone from the kitchen counter.

Yikes! She'd missed three calls and four texts from Reese. But an alert from her credit card company piqued her immediate interest. The Deep had issued a refund, which thrilled her in one way. Maybe Easy Ride really had wanted to make out with her after all, and didn't see it as a job duty. In fact, the whole session was free.

But she felt the potential story slip from her fingers as easily as the valet ticket had slipped away on the dance floor.

The visit had hinted at a possible story, even though she and her friend-for-hire didn't violate any laws. At least, not any she was aware of. She could still focus on the unsavory aspect of the business. The public gobbled up "unsavory" as easily as Lady gobbled up shrimp in aspic.

Besides, if she and Easy Ride went as far as they did within an hour, it could easily go all the way the next time. Maybe he'd even take her money. Maybe she could get in and out and wrap up the story before anything awful happened.

Awful, like being rejected. Except rejection hadn't seemed possible the other night.

As she began to entertain how "all the way" would feel with that particular animal, someone pounded on her front door.

Lady ripped out of Kirby's embrace, leaving a streak of scratches in her wake. No blood, thankfully, but the cat's claws left some impressive welts.

Kirby looked out the peephole, then swung the door open.

Reese wasn't alone. A very familiar and adorable rescue puppy stood next to her. Either the puppy had belonged to a decent owner at some point, or she was unusually self-disciplined.

Her best friend, by contrast, didn't look quite as calm.

"I've been calling and texting you all night," Reese practically screamed.

The poor thing slumped as if she hadn't slept in ages. Her already pale skin looked totally bleached out, along with her naturally blond eyebrows and hair. If it wasn't for her chocolate-brown eyes, she could pass for a ghost.

"I'm so sorry. Come in."

"You won't freakin' believe this, Kirby. My rescue Doberman got way too excited over having a foster sibling. He just wants to play, but he doesn't realize his strength. I tried putting the puppy in another room, but he knew she was there and wouldn't stop whimpering. All night long."

"Were the kennels full?"

"The ones I could reach, as were our usual foster families. Which is why I'm here."

"Reese—"

"I know I promised not to ask again. But please help me this time. I'll do the work in finding a suitable home. She needs food, shelter and a little tender loving care in the meantime. Nothing more."

Kirby exhaled a deep sigh and mustered the courage to say the two-letter word that always eluded her: no.

The crazy little puppy tilted her mop of a head and looked up, and the letters voluntarily transposed and expanded into a longer word and conditional commitment.

"Only if Lady approves."

Reese's shoulders visibly relaxed.

"Let her loose," Kirby said.

The puppy raced to the ottoman, straight into the black cat's domain.

Lady stared at this odd creature, with its open-mouth breathing and inebriated gait and slap-happy tail. She glared for a long time before taking a decisive swat, claws safely sheathed.

The puppy heeded the warning and wisely retreated.

"Okay. Lady can hold her own. Looks like the pup knows who's alpha," Kirby said.

Reese gave her a good long hug. That made two hugs in less than forty-eight hours. Three, if she counted Lady. And she definitely counted Lady.

"I don't suppose you brought any puppy food with you," Kirby said.

"Oh, no! In all the excitement, I forgot. I'll go get—"

"No worries. I'm headed to the store. You go home and get some sleep."

Reese nodded. "By the way, what should we name her?"

Naming the creature. A dangerous tactic because it became personal for them. It also became more personal for potential adopters.

"Baby," Kirby blurted out.

Reese seemed to consider it.

"Cute. Sounds like you've already given it some thought." Reese raised one eyebrow as if requesting confirmation.

"It's a nod to you. During the rescue, you said 'baby needs a bath.' I guess it stuck," Kirby said.

"Uh-huh."

Why didn't Reese believe her? Was she somehow giving away the real reason for the name? How "Baby Blue" had become a serious earworm, and how Easy Ride had moaned "Oh, baby," which sent her straight over the edge?

That had to stay a secret. She'd told Reese more than she should have about the undercover assignment, but only because Reese had provided the lead through a friend of a friend.

As soon as Reese left, Kirby finished pulling herself together. Only, when she glanced at herself in the mirror, something really did seem different.

She looked satisfied. Glowing. Even without a touch of makeup.

Furthermore, she knew exactly why.

KIRBY MUTTERED AN oath as she wrestled the shopping cart into semiforward motion.

Why did she always grab the one with a mutant wheel?

Usually, it was luck. This time, it was the worst kind of luck. All the other carts were scattered about the far end of the parking lot like so many cattle grazing in an open field. She couldn't summon the energy to corral a healthier one. Not without her morning jolt of caffeine.

Coffee. Puppy food. She could do this.

She pushed the oversized contraption forward, even though it argued loudly the entire way. All the while, she kept an eye out for the now-familiar hottie.

*Coffee. Puppy food. Fabian.*

Oh, and some tampons. Almost forgot about the near-empty box. Talk about averting a crisis.

Since the feminine hygiene aisle was the closest, she ambled down that one first, grabbing the appropriate product amid the sea of pastels.

Might as well get some ice cream, too, she thought, because the craving for sweets always preceded the dreaded monthly event. Who needed a calendar when, three days earlier, nothing but mint chip would do?

She almost passed the pet food aisle on the way to the frozen foods, but was able to wield the metallic monster to the left, where she grabbed some Puppy Chow. Next stop: Häagen-Dazs.

Two quart selections later, she figured she should offset the imminent diet damage with a salad while she was there.

So much for the grocery list.

The cart rebelled all the way toward the packaged salad display. But before she could quiet the beast, she spotted the gorgeous backside of a man.

With her libido still in overdrive, and her thoughts still replaying the touch and feel and smell of Easy Ride, was it any wonder her mind redrew him, right in front of her?

She shook her head at the similarities and even blinked a couple of times to dislodge them, but she couldn't look away. The view was amazing, which told her there were at least two men in the world who could raise her sexual desires from the dead.

The man's thick, almost-black hair had the same sultry bed-head appeal. His sculpted arms filled out his short-sleeve T-shirt very nicely. And those sweatpants hanging from his slender hips and über-toned ass confirmed his gender beyond a doubt. The combination caused a flush of heat to spread through her nervous stomach and pool between her thighs.

Her eyes feasted upon the man's form, tracing the outline of his hips, all the way up to those tanned, well-defined biceps.

If she wasn't mistaken, some ink peeked out from below the bottom of the sleeve.

The most intense yearning crashed down in hot waves inside her lower belly. She gulped back the excitement, or perhaps dread, that this could be the same man she had made out with. The same man who positioned himself on top of her and literally thrust her into a physical state she thought she'd never again visit.

Even though she had been mentally ready to chat with Fabian, she wasn't prepared for this. If she turned and ran as fast as she could, the noise from her cart would get everyone's attention. Including his. Abandoning her groceries wasn't an option. Maybe she could go a few more days without ice cream, but Baby needed food. Now.

Might as well say hello. Besides, perhaps it wasn't him. Perhaps her mind was playing cruel-but-mouthwatering tricks on her.

She stopped the cart a couple of feet to his right. Close enough to erase all doubts.

He looked up from the package he was studying.

"Am I in your way?" he asked while taking a polite step aside.

It seemed to take him a moment to recognize the total mess standing beside him. He returned the package of hearts of Romaine to the rack, then stepped forward and embraced her fully.

"Hey, you," he whispered.

As if the whole thing was out of her control, as if her arms insisted on returning the hug against her heart's admonishment that this must be a trap, she wrapped herself around him and absorbed his warmth and strength.

He pulled away while visually taking her in.

The sudden pang of regret for not having properly showered and at least applied lipstick and mascara snapped at her gut like a thick rubber band.

"What a coincidence. I've been thinking about you," he said.

Those baby blues of his concurred, and the subsequent smile produced the faintest crow's feet at the far edges.

Again, her heart sparred with her mind over the possible interpretations. Apparently, her mouth had another idea entirely.

"I thought about you, too. Once."

*Once, but nonstop.*

Now Easy Ride seemed to be trying to interpret her words.

"I hear you change tires. Could you take a look at this one?" she said, if only to distract him from her knee-jerk admission. She topped it off with her trademark smile as she pointed to the mutant wheel of her cart.

He shook his head.

"What? You do change tires, don't you?" Why did it suddenly feel as if she were back in high school?

"Your smile should be registered as a lethal weapon."

That confirmed it. She'd always known its power, even if she didn't understand it.

"I'm Adam, by the way."

"Kirby," she said as she initiated a handshake.

He cupped her hand in both of his instead. His hands were large and strong, yet soft and gentle. The whole thing sent a flood of tingles to her core as she recalled the way those hands had grabbed her rear and moved her against his hardness.

He gave her hand a quick squeeze before releasing it, then reached into her cart.

"Hey, get your own Puppy Chow," she said.

He simply smiled and transferred her groceries, including the bright pink box. If he knew what he'd touched, he didn't indicate having any issues about it.

Once the merge was complete, he turned his cart around, patted the handle bar as an invitation for her to join and together they pushed.

His hands and arms looked so strong and capable

compared to hers, and his body radiated a yummy warmth—a curled-up-together-in-a-cashmere-blanket kind of warmth—as he pressed against her side.

It always amazed her how guys could wear short sleeves in cool weather and somehow retain so much body heat, whereas she remained bone-cold beneath long sleeves.

"What, exactly, are we doing?" she asked.

"Besides relieving the other customers of the noise? We're shopping together."

His mouth was so close, so soft-looking, so kissable, her mouth practically watered to taste him again.

Her whole morning oozed temptation. Speaking of which…

"We better shop fast. My ice cream is melting. Things could get messy," she said.

*I could get messy.*

Silence accompanied their walk toward wherever he was headed, but for some odd reason the whole scenario felt comfortable instead of awkward. As if they'd been shopping together for aeons, and this was nothing more than another trip to the store, which begged a certain question.

"Do you come here often?" she asked.

"Apparently not often enough," he said, then shot her a wink and a smile. "Actually, Fabian and I work out next door at Six-Pax. Just got through, as a matter of fact."

She grinned at how beautifully her plan to run into Fabian had failed so miserably.

"That's a relief. I was worried you'd come here specifically to stalk me, since you couldn't stop thinking about me and all." She nudged his arm to indicate she wasn't serious.

"You'd know if I were. I don't hide behind salad displays. I'm more of a get-straight-to-the-point kind of stalker. Seeing you again was a nice bonus."

"Likewise. So, what's on your shopping list?" she asked.

He stopped the cart, bit his bottom lip and looked at her. As if he needed something personal. Something unmentionable.

*Condoms.*

"Toothpaste," he finally said.

She pointed toward the far end of the store. Together, they guided their mutual cart.

If she hadn't managed to brush her teeth before coming to the store, she might've thought their destination was a not-so-subtle hint.

Adam forced the basket to a halt in front of the toothbrushes.

"Soft, medium or hard?" he asked.

She pushed back the erotic image he had provoked with the final word, then swallowed. Hard.

"What?"

"I'm buying a toothbrush for you to keep at my place in case you take me up on my offer to cook dinner for you. Tonight, if you're available."

"Oh."

What she felt like saying was, this was moving awfully fast. It felt as rocky and disjointed as the mutant wheel of her abandoned shopping cart. He hadn't lied about being a straight-to-the-point sort of guy.

He shook his head and looked at the floor in blatant embarrassment. She wished she hadn't sounded so underwhelmed.

"I don't mean to pressure you or put you on the spot," he said as he looked up. "But I'd like to see you again, outside of the club. Maybe this was a corny way to approach the subject, but I hadn't expected to run into you."

"Are you saying your dialogue is usually scripted?" She softened the accusation with a smile.

A quivering, nervous smile. It had been so long since a man pursued her like this. Much less a drop-dead gorgeous man.

"Not usually. Am I being too direct? I can still be your shoulder to cry on, if that's what you want or need."

*If you only knew.*

Then again, there was no way to really know someone without a time investment. And, if she didn't take a chance every now and again, she'd miss out on everything. And everyone.

"Look, Kirby, what happened between us at the club was unprofessional on my part. I've never done that with a client, unlike some of the other guys. I mean, the stories those sofas could tell…"

His confession might as well have been a slap upside her dreamy little head. She'd momentarily forgotten what those guys must be doing for a living, much less what she needed to do to earn hers.

Yet, a part of her needed to mend her broken past above all else. So much so, she was willing to put herself into the hands of this total stranger. Besides, he didn't strike her as the serious type, which would definitely complicate things. But getting to know him even a little better might lead to some revelations about the club that she wouldn't be able to get inside those protected walls.

He was patient, if anything. He gave her time to think.

No pressure, like he promised. Nothing but an impromptu invitation into his home for dinner. And a place to hang her toothbrush.

"Soft," she said. "I like my toothbrush soft."

He turned and picked out a pink one with soft bristles. With a raise of one eyebrow, he officially popped the question.

And with a nod of her head, she answered.

*SOFT.*

Like her lips, her hair, her skin.

Had he really done this? Something so utterly corny and bold with a woman he barely knew?

Apparently so. It was as if he couldn't help himself. It had been so long since he'd felt an attraction for anyone, much less one so intense and unexpected.

Adam tossed the toothbrush into the cart, alongside her feminine products, puppy food and melting ice cream.

"Is there anything else you need?" she asked.

"Can't think of a thing."

Except, yeah, he needed something. But ravaging her luscious body in a grocery store wasn't an option. So, together, they headed toward the checkout line.

As they walked, he thought about how she'd tried to book another session. He couldn't let that happen. It came down to more than his desire to see her again. This was about professional preservation and adhering to the club's cardinal rule. The way she'd said the word *soft* had turned him anything but. This one, he was powerless against.

Didn't hurt that his grandfather had met his own wife in a grocery store. How they both reached for the same head of iceberg lettuce and it felt as though he'd been pulled under by the strongest current. And how the whole thing spurred a request for a date within minutes, and a marriage proposal within weeks.

True love can happen that fast, and in the strangest of

places, even though what he felt at the moment wasn't love. But if there was one takeaway from his grandfather's schmaltzy story, it was to never go into a relationship with preconceived notions of how it should begin.

If this thing with Kirby progressed, his story would unspool much differently than his grandfather's. In fact, he wouldn't be able to repeat it to Henry in its entirety. The part about meeting in the lettuce section, however, was a definite keeper.

*What the hell?*

Where had those thoughts come from? Next thing, he'd be visualizing how she'd look walking down the church aisle, rather than the grocery aisle.

Adam dismissed the ridiculous train of thought and began stacking their groceries on the conveyer belt.

She reached into her purse.

"I've got this," he said as he placed a hand over hers.

He'd do anything to stack the odds in his favor. Not that he wanted her to feel obligated to him in any way.

Well, maybe a little.

"I can't let you pay."

"Sure you can. You have only a couple of items. I'll hold the ice cream for ransom. That way, if you back out, I'll have it to console me."

Then again, if she did follow through on his invite, what would he cook for dinner? Not exactly his finest skill, although he could grill a steak like nobody's business.

Adam helped the sacker further separate his items from Kirby's. It had been a while since he'd handled a pink box for a woman. She didn't seem entirely comfortable about it, which he found charming. He practically sensed her discomfort as he peeled off some bills to pay for everything.

Last thing he wanted to do was come across as a controlling son of a bitch, but he wanted to do this. Still, there was a fine line between chivalry and sexism these days. In fact, the line was invisible to him, so his other senses had to navigate.

He walked Kirby to her car, and challenged the invisible line once again by opening the car door for her.

She tossed her grocery bag in the backseat, then leaned against the side of the car.

He closed the space between them, slipped his hands beneath her orange jersey and rested his palms on her hips, allowing his thumbs to cop a feel of her warm skin.

She looked even lovelier in the daylight without makeup. He easily imagined how her unleashed hair would look against his pillowcase, first thing in the morning. At the thought of how he might actually get to find out, his cock twitched and he felt the damn thing growing hard.

He glanced around the parking lot. Other people kept busy leading their own lives. Not that he would mind if anyone happened to see them standing this close, like lovers.

Her breathing seemed to deepen as she ran her hands up his arms, caressing him with the softest velvet skin known to man. She lifted the edge of his sleeve and studied his tattoo. Her touch soothed the residual humiliation.

"I'd love to know the story behind this," she said.

He winced. That conversation would definitely have to be scripted.

Or, maybe not. He wanted to know more about her. If this unexpected relationship lasted beyond tomorrow morning, he'd pursue full disclosure.

"Maybe I'll tell you when I pick you up tonight."

Her breath audibly hitched when he pressed into her a little deeper.

"I'd rather drive to your place," she said.

Adam would ordinarily assume he'd crossed the invisible line, if it weren't for the way she pressed into him as she spoke.

A slight breeze blew a loose strand of hair across her eyes, and she tried to blink it away.

He reached up, brushed it out of her face and tucked the stray strand behind her ear.

"Any special meaning?" he asked as he touched the silver horseshoe adorning only one of her lobes.

"It's supposed to bring good luck. Seems to be working."

He wasn't about to disagree.

"Would you have even more luck if you wore both of them?" Although, he wasn't sure how much better it could get, at least for him.

She felt the bare lobe.

"Oh. I always forget to take these off at night. The other one is probably on top of the pillow. I'll try to be fully accessorized tonight. When I drive to your place."

He noticed a faint splattering of freckles across her nose, and the familiar soap-and-water freshness of her skin.

Of course she'd want a way to leave. Hell, whenever he had a daughter, he hoped she'd use a little common sense about such things. And he sure wouldn't raise a son who violated women's boundaries.

"Understood," he said. "But this might change your mind. I live on the outskirts of town."

"You can check my tires first. What's your address? I'll leave a copy of the info at home in case I go missing."

"I'll give you my address when you give me your

phone number." He retrieved his cell phone from his pocket, typed in her name and handed the phone to her.

He studied her face as she punched. And punched.

She bit her bottom lip, smiled with her eyes and handed the phone back to him.

He pressed into her again and went in for a kiss to seal the deal.

She allowed his lips and tongue to explore her own before she returned the favor. After a few glorious moments, they relaxed into a loose embrace.

For him, it was the best kiss so far. Liv hadn't exactly spoiled him when it came to public displays of affection in any form. And he was a big fan of PDA.

To be fair, Liv had been more than affectionate behind closed doors. Problem was, she was also affectionate behind other men's doors.

But that was the past. What was happening right now was exactly what he needed.

Judging by the way Kirby ran her hands down his back and leaned forward for a full-body embrace, the PDA was good for her.

At least he hoped it was because he was trying to stack the odds even more in his favor, all the while knowing that this kiss could be their last.

It hadn't been lost on him how she hesitated when he'd handed her his phone, and even re-input her own number with slow, deliberate strokes. Then, she seemed to delete part of it and input a different number.

Question was, had Kirby changed it to the correct number, or was she giving him a fake one?

# 5

KIRBY'S GOOFY SMILE must have looked beyond crazed. Both her cheeks ached from the nonstop strain of unbridled happiness. Adam had put the smile there with his embrace, his kisses, the invitation to dinner at his house.

Baby's enthusiastic greeting pushed her smile to even more extremes the moment she walked into her loft.

Lady simply inventoried the ridiculous scene from a window ledge across the room, then turned her feline attention to the cacophony of traffic on the midtown street below.

Kirby poured some Puppy Chow into a bowl and placed it on the ground.

"Here you go."

Baby ravaged the offering. Her little tail wagged so hard it made her whole backside move back and forth like a manic metronome.

"Now. Finally. My turn."

Except, wait, she'd forgotten the most important item. The coffee.

She'd been totally distracted. Surprisingly, she didn't feel the least bit tired anymore. Maybe Adam could replace her caffeine addiction.

Or create a whole new one.

A wave of warmth oozed across her skin at the thought of those baby blue eyes taking their time with her. Savoring her. Deepening to a slightly darker hue after kissing her. Watching her input her phone number, then punch it in again. Out of nervousness, she'd transposed two digits and had to start over.

Her number was now on his phone, she was reasonably sure of it. This gorgeous man with an equally gorgeous hard-on for her had her number.

Desire tugged at her core as she recalled the way his hardness felt against her thin yoga pants, hitting the most sensitive spot as he so effortlessly seemed to do. In between carnal thoughts, she wrestled with the reality of what he did for a living, and how he seemed to be hiding something else.

The tattoo on his biceps? Clearly a correction or cover-up, based on how the tangled threads of ink within the horse's mane looked slightly darker in the light, as if they didn't belong.

She reached into the shower and turned the knob to hot.

For the first time in a long time, she watched herself undress. Her clothes hadn't been deceiving. She had shed a few pounds without even trying.

Stress. The best weight-loss pill she'd ever swallowed.

Yet, Adam hinted that he liked her curves. His body didn't lie the first time, or this last time.

The bittersweetness of it caught in her throat as she struggled to accept this as a valid truth. She was still sexy, despite how her failed marriage had made her feel.

No sooner had she lathered up her hair than her cell phone rang.

Tingles two-stepped across her flesh at the prospect

of him calling so soon. The dance was swept along by rivulets of warm water as she rinsed out the shampoo.

"Please, please, please be Adam," she whispered as she applied deep conditioner to her hair.

Clearly, some of the sentiments he had expressed in the club were for real. He was under no obligation to see her outside work. Much less buy and keep a toothbrush for her at his house. He'd even insisted on paying for her groceries. Aside from her father, no man had ever done that. In fact, quite the opposite.

Three minutes later, she couldn't endure the suspense any longer, so she rinsed the deep conditioner from her hair.

She dried off, wrapped her hair in the same towel and walked naked across the room to hopefully find a voice mail from Adam. She even managed to add a little sway. It had been a long time since she felt capable, much less worthy, of such a seductive movement.

The missed number looked vaguely familiar. The caller hadn't left a message. She should have insisted he give her his number again, as well.

No sooner had she thought this, than another call came in from the same number.

*Answer it...*

"This is Kirby."

"Hey. I'm glad you picked up."

The voice sounded a bit too high to be Adam.

It could be the reception. Besides, who else would be saying such things? It wasn't as if men were beating down her door.

"I'm glad I picked up, too," she said.

Nothing but a strange, singular chuckle on the other end.

Maybe she hadn't immediately recognized her ex-husband's voice, but his bravado was unmistakable.

"What do you want, Tim? I'm busy."

"Too busy to talk to me for one minute?"

It was her turn to chuckle. Why was she even still on the line?

"I didn't call to fight," he said. "I want to tell you something before you hear it elsewhere."

"What? You've got a terminal illness? I'll break out the Dom Pérignon."

"I deserve that. I wasn't the best husband."

"Talk about an understatement."

"Yeah. I know. But I've changed. I got some therapy, like you always wanted me to do."

The air conditioner kicked on, and she didn't have so much as a towel to protect her. Every inch of her flesh goose-bumped and her teeth were on the verge of chattering.

This was the last thing she needed. He'd tried to get back together twice already but refused couples' therapy each time. The damage was done, and he had never been man enough to undo it. Until now, apparently.

But she'd made the mistake of trusting him once. She'd made the stupid, stupid, stupid decision to turn down a golden investigative journalist opportunity in Chicago and follow him to Texas instead, only to have him turn her down. Financially. Emotionally.

Physically.

Besides, she was finally getting the sexual validation that her ex-husband had denied her.

"I'm sorry, Tim. I'm not willing to give us another chance. I've met someone."

The long pause that followed was supremely gratifying.

"Wow. Kirby. Awesome news. I'm happy for you."

Funny. She didn't note any sarcasm in his voice. And he had quite the capacity for it.

"I'm happy, too."

It was the truth. The thought of seeing Adam again sent flurries of pleasure straight down to her naked sex, even though Tim's voice battled to take them away.

"That's great, Kirby. I hope you can be happy for me, too."

She shivered again, from the inside out. So he hadn't called to get back together. All of a sudden, she felt beyond ridiculous.

"What did you want to tell me?" she asked.

"I'm getting married," he said without missing a beat.

The words landed like a sucker punch to the back.

"Right, Tim. You said you never wanted to be married, and you proved it. The second time won't be any different."

"I believe it will. Amber is great. I've never wanted anything so much in my life, and she and I both want children."

Tears welled in Kirby's eyes as fast and furious as a tsunami, but she refused to let him hear so much as a gulp or sniffle. He'd never been that excited about her, yet he didn't want anyone else to have her, either. He had never wanted children, although he made her believe otherwise until after the vows. Now, someone wonderful had changed his mind?

She couldn't run to the bathroom and grab another towel quick enough. Couldn't wrap it tightly enough around her to mask the humiliation she felt.

In a single instant, her ex had set her back, and undid all of the goodness she'd experienced from Adam.

There had been tender moments with Tim, in the beginning. Passion-filled kisses followed by heated lovemaking sessions, although she didn't remember them with any intensity. Had time dulled those memories, or were her new memories with Adam that much stronger? Not to mention so much hotter.

No matter. Her relationship with Tim had ended in the most devastating way. The same way it could easily end with Adam.

Kirby pressed End Call without so much as a comment or goodbye. Didn't matter whether Tim thought she was happy or sad, strong or weak. She didn't care about him or his future. Point was, he'd called after all this time for the sole purpose of reminding her how unwanted she had been, which accomplished nothing except to tear open the old wound with an angry vengeance.

If only she'd given Adam a fake number, she might avoid another possible heartbreak. She could have, *should* have, kept it strictly business and stayed focused on the story. What had she been thinking?

The telephone rang again.

She recognized all the numbers now, if not the order they appeared on the screen.

*Adam*.

She set down the unanswered phone, went to curl into a fetal position on top of her bed and retreated into the dark emotional chasm in which she'd resided for the past year. In the distance, the new voice mail alert chimed. That didn't mean she had to play it.

But the longer she stayed motionless and disconnected, the more it felt as though history was repeating itself. Tim had denied her, physically. Now, his call was making her doubt Adam's affection, robbing her of pleasure once again.

Not to mention, if she allowed this to drag her under,

she'd screw up a golden career opportunity. Just like before. Because of Tim.

At that, she bolted upright. She was clear on what needed to be done, and it didn't involve wallowing in self-pity. *Get the damn story.*

And stop questioning any pleasure that comes with it.

ADAM PARKED OFF the main street and hoofed it down the unpaved road to Becker Farms.

The scene of the crime. Except, the only crimes committed had been those against him, beginning with false accusations of sexual misconduct.

As if he'd give Madison Kelly a second glance. He hadn't even been her instructor, for Christ's sake. He'd never once been alone with her. While Liv had been busy cheating on him, Madison Kelly had been fabricating some private fantasies that played out all too publicly.

It still perplexed the hell out of him at how Madison had even come up with such claims. How she had mistaken verbal kindness for physical advances. She was the one who flirted with him. Pursued him. Hell, he should have been the one to cry foul.

Everyone believed her version of the story. Took her side. That was the crappiest part of the whole damn thing.

Boiling fury pumped through his veins and fueled his steps, but reality stopped him cold. The fence before him wasn't jumpable. To complicate matters, they'd installed some sort of security gate, complete with camera.

Fortunately, he knew another way in. Unless they had blocked it after evicting him from the property.

Adam skirted the perimeter and dodged the camera sweeps until he reached the back of one of the covered arenas and located the gate with the torn wiring.

The existing tear in the fence allowed him enough room to enter if he held his breath. His newly ripped muscles almost prevented him from slipping through. However, a Houdini-worthy squeeze later, he was in.

Sweet success.

Or was it? Donald Becker had incorrectly pinned the theft of some Hermès saddles on Adam, which meant trespassing was probably the dumbest idea he'd ever had. But he needed to see Daisy. The Arabian mare had been on his mind, and she'd long been tattooed over his heart. Still, ink was a poor substitute for the real deal.

He pulled his Stetson lower on his forehead and kept his head down while walking past the riders who practiced drills in the larger of the two covered arenas. No sign of Becker.

Adam remained cautiously optimistic. Becker traveled eight months of the year to horse shows and rodeos and auctions, leaving all the responsibility on his lovely wife, Trish. Who knew how she felt about Adam? He had been kicked out so fast, he hadn't had a chance to talk to her.

Thankfully, Daisy was in her stall, which had a faint ammonia smell. *Urine.*

If he were still here, the stalls would be immaculate, which triggered an unfortunate impulse to kick back against the accusations, once again. Fight for his reputation and his previous life here, rather than running off to the Emerald Coast.

But that proverbial horse had already galloped into the sunset. Besides, his grandfather couldn't stop talking about Destin. Adam hadn't seen the man so excited about anything in ages.

"Hey, girl. Remember me?"

Daisy rubbed her muzzle against his open palm. No reintroduction necessary.

It was all he could do to choke back the emotion as he retrieved a small apple from his shirt pocket and fed her a treat.

The bossy steps of the resident Pembroke Welsh corgi flitted around the edge of Adam's awareness right before Sergeant announced his presence with a gigantic bark.

Adam turned and scooped him up. The dog's licking and tail thrashing offered undeniable assurance he hadn't been forgotten by this little horse herder, either. In fact, he could practically feel the needle prick of another tattoo. This time, in Sergeant's honor.

As if the corgi hadn't drawn enough attention, Adam's cell phone rang. He hadn't put it on vibrate because he didn't want to miss Kirby's call. He'd almost lost all hope that she'd given him the correct number.

He set down Sergeant and retrieved his phone while the corgi invisibly lassoed his ankles with nonstop circling.

His heart did a somersault when he saw the name he'd programmed in.

"Adam here."

"Hey there. It's Kirby."

Damn if a huge grin didn't spread across his face at the sound of her voice, and a definite heat rushed to his cock. It was as if his entire body was possessed.

"Thanks for calling me back."

Silence. *Uh-oh...*

"About dinner tonight..." she said.

He placed a hand on the stall door and steadied himself against the forthcoming kick in the ego. His somersaulting heart paused, as well.

Should he let her bow out gracefully, or should he

play the only card that could possibly work in this particular situation: the guilt card?

Then again, what did he have to lose?

*My focus. That's what.*

He didn't have any business starting up with her when he might not be in town much longer. In fact, he should accept this as a blessing in disguise. Maybe follow up with the job offer instead. Keep his priorities straight, so the universe didn't get mixed messages. But he couldn't seem to get her out of his stubborn mind.

"Yeah. I've been thinking about tonight, too. About how I can't wait to see you, Kirby. And hold you."

*And kiss you.*

He couldn't tell whether the subsequent sigh was a good sigh or a stressed one, but his bet was on the latter. Maybe he should give himself a good kick in the ass to go with the boot she was about to administer.

Instead, he loosened the reins. "But if you can't come, I understand."

"I was going to say, about tonight, is there anything I can bring? A wedge of cheese? A bottle of wine? A Maltese-terrier mix?"

"A what?"

"Sorry. I'm fostering a rescue dog and I can't find anyone to take care of her tonight. She should be fine through dinner, under the watchful eye of my alpha cat. But I'm afraid I won't be able to stay long enough to break in that toothbrush."

Adam exhaled. Had she really been stressing over this? He was crazy about animals. Dogs in particular with cats coming in a close second. He vowed to adopt a pet the minute he got his shit together, which looked like never.

In fact, part of his brain entertained the idea of steal-

ing Sergeant. If Becker wanted to accuse him of being a
thief, he might as well get something out of it.

"Adam, are you there?"

If he were honest, he'd have to say his thoughts were
all over the place. As far as the dilemma about her res-
cue-dog situation, the answer was a little too easy.

"Bring the pup. The cat, too, if you'd like."

He proceeded to spell out his address, along with directions, then ended the call.

This good news meant he'd need to wrap up his clan-
destine meeting with Daisy and Sergeant, and pick up a
steak and a swordfish filet at the market. Maybe some
asparagus, too. How hard could that be to grill?

Oh, and hearts of Romaine. For luck, if nothing else.
Better yet, a head of iceberg. All of a sudden, everything
seemed possible. At least, right up until the moment he
turned to find Donald Becker standing less than ten feet
away, arms crossed and flanked by two men in blue.

*Fuck.*

"You're not supposed to be here, Adam. What are
you doing?"

"I'm visiting Daisy and Sergeant. What does it look
like? Feel free to frisk me for any missing saddles."

He hadn't meant to be so sarcastic, but his bravado
was overcompensating for his feet, which were shaking
in his Lucchese boots. It would be his luck to get arrested
and not be there when Kirby arrived.

*If* she arrived.

"Leave now and I won't press charges for trespassing," Becker said.

"You got it. But since I have your undivided attention, please enlighten me as to why you think I stole
the saddles."

Becker paused, and Adam wondered how much he'd

screwed up any defamation case he might have had. His lawyer, Bernard, could be as patient as a saint. But he'd probably drop Adam as a client after this latest stunt.

"Okay. I'll tell you why, although I think it's rather obvious. You were the only one with a key to the restricted part of the tack room."

"No one has been inside the vault in the past year?"

"Not a soul. Not Trish. Not even me until the other day, to take my annual inventory."

"Flimsy evidence, if you ask me. Feel free to stop by my house and look around for the missing saddles. It's the same house where you and Trish stayed for five weeks after that fire destroyed your home. I believe you still have a key. Maybe I'm the one who should take inventory."

That said, Adam strode past Becker, looking him directly in the eye the entire time.

As suspected, Becker looked down at his feet.

*Asshole.*

Adam bypassed the cops, but braced himself for the cold slap of handcuffs nonetheless.

The hardest part was walking past Daisy and leaving Sergeant behind, knowing he would never be back.

As he walked off the property, he wanted more than ever to live an improved version of his old life. A version where he called the shots. Wild Indigo made Becker's place look like a dump. He could visualize himself there now, which made it even more imperative that he get the job and get the hell out of Texas.

Except for one minor problem. He couldn't visualize saying goodbye to Kirby.

KIRBY SKIPPED LUNCH ALTOGETHER. She didn't even trust saltines to stay down at this point.

Was she really going through with this? And had she made Baby an accomplice in her questionable judgment? She still needed useable footage of the club. Any illegal activity had to be outed. And she didn't want to raise suspicion by booking time with him now, much less with someone else. That could present a huge problem.

But Adam's voice alone had both soothed and aroused her. She'd also made the mistake of slipping back into her yoga pants and jersey, which still smelled faintly of vanilla and pine.

In the end, her longing body convinced her hesitant mind that she could do this. Besides, a more relaxed setting might encourage more openness. Adam had information. He said it himself.

*The stories those sofas could tell...*

At least one truth was obvious. She couldn't base the rest of her life on what had happened with her abusive, screwed-up ex-husband. In fact, she felt rather sorry for his fiancée.

"Better her than me."

Even saying it out loud made it easier for her to breathe, because it was the truth, which was exactly why she wanted to be a reporter. Tim's call still served as a reminder to let her head take the lead, because her heart was a terrible fact-checker.

She was able to do that at work. Why, then, was the truth so hard to accept when it came to her personal life?

She closed her eyes and tried to look at this situation with Adam objectively, as she would a news story. With each subsequent revelation, easier breaths followed.

Truth. Adam wasn't Tim.

Truth. She would be spending the night with Adam tonight.

Truth. He wasn't going to reject her.

*At least, not so soon.*

"Shut *up*!" she screamed at her stubborn inner voice, which sucked the optimism right out of her every time. So much for being objective.

Someone knocked on the door, interrupting her process of overthinking.

Had she yelled that loudly? If so, how could the neighbors be on her doorstep so soon? She looked out the peephole, then flung open the door.

"I didn't say anything, I promise," Reese said.

"You heard me?"

"Uh. Yeah. Me and all the folks at the Starbucks on the corner. Are you alone?"

"Alone with my thoughts. Call 911."

"No need. I'm here to save you." Reese held up a bag of Puppy Chow.

"I bought some this morning, but thanks."

Kirby hefted the bag from Reese anyway. All thirty pounds of it, which could only mean one thing.

"No leads on a forever home?"

Not that it would happen so quickly. Could take weeks, if ever, even when the creature was as adorable and well-behaved as Baby.

"Not yet. There's something else I need to discuss with you." Reese made herself comfortable on the couch.

"If this is a Häagen-Dazs discussion, I don't have any." Kirby tried to conceal her smile but did a lousy job of it.

"Obviously I'm not the only one with something to share. Please tell me that satisfied smirk of yours has nothing to do with the guy you met at The Deep."

"Well, aren't you a bucket of ice water."

"Tell me you did not sleep with him."

Kirby bit the inside of her cheek, then retreated to the kitchen and retrieved two cans of Fresca from the fridge.

Lady simply watched from her perch.

"I did not sleep with him." She handed one of the cans to Reese but remained standing.

"What a relief."

"Why? You're the one who said I should go for it."

"I know. But I suggested it before I talked to Becky directly. You know, the friend of the friend who tipped me off about the place?"

"I know. And multiple thanks to all of you for the lead."

"You'll thank me more for what I'm about to tell you. Those guys aren't just bad boys. They're actually bad."

"Isn't that the point of my investigation?"

"I suppose. But apparently some of them are pretty high-pressure. As in, desperate-car-salesman level. At least one of them can't even get a job selling used cars because of his criminal record."

Kirby took a long sip of the cold soda to wash down what Reese had force-fed her, then dropped onto the sofa.

"Is your friend implying that women have been raped, and that one or more of the guys have been convicted?" The whole concept made her bones ache, straight down to the marrow. That would take her investigation to a whole other level.

"No, not that. Becky is hot and heavy with her club guy. He practically bragged about his felony conviction, laundering money for the Mafia up in New York State. Yet, she keeps going there to see him. I seriously question her taste in men and her judgment in general."

"Did she mention his name or moniker?"

"I'm pretty sure I heard her say 'John.'"

"That's not my guy's name. Not even close."

Yet, some major red flags had been raised. Kirby hadn't even thought to ask for his last name so she could check public records, which was an odd error in judgment—both professionally and personally. But she hadn't exactly been thinking clearly.

"Felony convictions aside, it sounds like some serious pressure is being served inside the club. Or maybe some serious seduction. I'm more than a little worried for you," Reese said.

Adam had been pretty forward, come to think of it. Yet, she had welcomed it. She needed it. Any and all seduction was consensual.

"I guess things like that happen in those types of places. Doesn't mean it will happen to me, but I don't want it happening to someone else. That's why I'm going there. To stop anyone who's taking advantage."

"I know you're smart. But those guys know what to say. They're like unlicensed therapists. Even though you might be willing, physically, you need to protect yourself emotionally."

"I'm a big girl. And, don't judge me, but I also happen to have a date tonight. With a big, bad boy."

"Well, okay," Reese said. "But remember, I'm here for you if you need anything. I owe you a big favor for taking care of Baby anyway."

No admonishment or trying to talk Kirby out of it. Not that Reese's opinion would have affected her decision.

But Reese had reminded her of what she detested most. False flattery. Mercenary men seducing women out of their hard-earned money, as well as their panties. Taking every conceivable advantage.

How could she reconcile the fact that Adam was one of those men?

# 6

Kirby pulled into the driveway of the sprawling ranch-style home. It wasn't at all what she expected of a man in his profession.

It was so much better.

And much more traditional, yet with contemporary elements, such as an expanse of windows separated by horizontal slats of dark wood and occasional gray stone treatments. Having lived in apartments or loft complexes most of her life, she only dreamed of such a place.

She double-checked the address again. Slowly. This was definitely it. Acres of land included.

Baby had been so quiet on the long drive into this heavily wooded, tucked-away edge of the city, she'd almost forgotten the puppy was in the car. Even though Lady had been invited, Kirby left her behind as an excuse to get back home in the morning and not be tempted to overstay her welcome.

The moment Kirby opened the car door, Baby barked excitedly.

"Maybe you'll have a home like this someday."

*Maybe we both will.*

As Baby continued to bark, Kirby practically purred.

Every inch of her ached with the anticipation of Adam's touch. She wetted her lips at the thought of being kissed again.

She managed to pull herself together despite her deliciously messy thoughts. If she were a quart of Häagen-Dazs, she'd be completely melted. And the night was just beginning.

With Baby in tow, Kirby proceeded up the wooden steps and onto a porch that wrapped around the home's sharp angles. She rang the bell and then turned to survey the property, which was quiet and lovely beneath the warm blanket of sunset.

If anything, it was too quiet. The large fenced-in field on one side of the house was as motionless as a photograph. A dark, abandoned stable appeared as though it had seen better days. Happier days.

She recognized the soothing sound of a Woodstock wind chime in the distance and imagined waking up to such a sound every morning.

The unlocking and opening of the door caused Baby to launch into a full-body wag.

No wonder. The man who stood on the other side of the threshold was enough to stir every inch of Kirby's being.

She took a top-to-bottom inventory of the masculine masterpiece in front of her. Glorious bed-head, muscles straining against a black T-shirt, one sculpted hand gripping a white flour-sack dishcloth while the other held open the door, the promise of his well-endowed manhood soon straining against black dress slacks, Baby licking his bare feet.

*Bare feet?*

Baby's smooth little tongue must have tickled because he laughed and attempted to sidestep the amorous fur ball.

"I knew I forgot something. Please, come in," he said, careful not to step on the puppy, who was obviously as taken with him as Kirby was, if not more so.

Adam tossed the dishcloth over his shoulder, scooped up Baby and took Kirby's hand, shutting the door with a barefoot back kick.

He led them through a foyer, into a great room and open kitchen.

She breathed in his clean scent of vanilla and pine as the large, wood-burning fireplace crackled in harmony with some contemporary jazz coming from the corner of the room.

The front of the house had promised spectacular views, and the rest of the home backed up that promise. Windows were everywhere, including on three sides of the kitchen, which looked out to tall trees and thick brush.

Adam set down Baby, patted the seat of a bar stool for Kirby and proceeded to pull two wineglasses from a cupboard and place them on the island in front of her. Expensive wineglasses, at that, even though she would gladly sip boxed wine from a plastic cup with this particular man.

"Red, white, or rosé?" he asked.

*Soft, medium, or hard?* Always so willing to please her.

She gulped back the thoughts of what else he might ask, if they moved this from the kitchen to the bedroom. She felt perfectly comfortable telling him how to please her in the oral hygiene or wine department. But in bed? That would be a different story.

"I'm partial to red, but I suppose it depends on what we're having for dinner," she said.

What, exactly, were they having for dinner?

"I'm preparing surf and turf, so the wine can go any which way. Don't let the cabernet glasses influence your decision. They're all I have. Or I can open a bottle of each. No rules tonight."

"How do *you* feel about red?" she asked. "This shouldn't be a unilateral decision."

"I prefer red, too."

He walked over to a Sub-Zero and scanned his inventory, which looked quite impressive from her vantage point.

"Is there anything I can do to help?" she asked as he effortlessly uncorked a bottle of Caymus Reserve.

Although she wasn't a connoisseur, she knew the bottle he selected wasn't the kind one would find in the boxed-wine aisle.

He poured them both a glass and handed one to her, then lifted his.

"A toast. To our first official date," he said.

She silently raised her glass.

Everything seemed perfect at the moment.

*Too perfect.*

She summoned her inner reporter, and admonished her heart to take a backseat. Or, at the very least, ride shotgun. Questions needed to be asked, but the timing had to be right.

Meanwhile, Baby ran amok, getting into who knew what.

"Sorry. She's obviously excited to be here," Kirby said.

He set his glass down and turned his attention to

something behind him. "I'm excited she's here, too. But I'm more excited over you."

The wine proceeded to warm her, along with his deep voice and the sweet words that went with it.

After grabbing a tray, he walked around the counter.

"Join me outside while I add the fish to the grill. The steak should be ready soon."

She set down her wineglass and eased off the bar stool as he disappeared through some sliding glass doors at the far end of the great room.

Baby followed him instead of waiting for her.

When Kirby reached for her glass again, it nearly toppled. And right on top of some paperwork he'd left on the counter.

Not a good place for anything white. Not with her around. Normally she had two left feet, but when she was nervous she had two left hands, as well. Although she wouldn't dream of taking the liberty of moving the paperwork, she couldn't help but notice it looked like some sort of legal document. A rather thick one.

"Adam Drake versus Becker Farms." A lawsuit of some kind.

Since he was listed first, he would be the plaintiff rather than the defendant. That was somewhat comforting. Not to mention, she finally had his last name.

The desire to turn the pages made her fingers itch, but she'd taken long enough. Besides, it didn't seem to involve The Deep and, therefore, wouldn't affect her story. Yet, it could have a lot to do with the type of man he was.

WHAT WAS TAKING her so long?

Adam alternately monitored the sliding glass door, the swordfish and the steak both sizzling on the grill and rapidly reaching perfection. This was one dinner he did not intend to burn.

He had a long history of burning dinners, and Liv had never let him forget it. She did have plenty of room to talk, being such an excellent cook herself. But Adam would rather eat corn chips and bean dip with Kirby than endure such scrutiny from a woman again.

Then it struck him how he'd set himself up for such a scenario by offering to cook dinner.

What was that saying about doing the same thing over and over and expecting different results?

*Right. Insanity.*

Kirby walked through the patio doors, rescuing him from his little trip down not-so-wonderful-memory lane.

Yeah, he definitely was a big fan of red. She looked incredible in her long, cherry-red figure-hugging dress with slits up both sides, offering quick and easy access to the heavens.

"Sorry for making you wait. I took off mine so we'd be on equal footing." She pointed downward.

Even her bare feet were sexy. She'd taken off her shoes, and he didn't even have to seduce her out of them.

"That looks and smells delicious," she said.

"So do you," he countered.

Sweet and clean. What a contrast to his thoughts, which were more along the lines of naughty and messy.

"What kind of fish are we having?" she asked.

"Texas swordfish. Even better than ones caught off the Keys, in my opinion. But Florida has the best beaches, hands down."

Might as well introduce the topic. At some point, he would have to tell her. At least, he hoped there would be a reason to do so. But whether or not the job offer came through, he'd like to see her again.

"I'm not a big fan. I burn, even with maximum SPF," she said.

*Well, damn.*

"Too bad, I bet those beaches would love you. I can picture you there. Maybe beneath one of those big umbrellas."

"Oh, really? Am I wearing a string bikini, by chance?"

He reached up and touched one of her earrings.

"No. Nothing except these. I see you found the mate," he said.

"I sure did. I suppose that means I'll have a little extra luck tonight."

"Trust me. You don't need the earrings. Not with me."

She lowered her head.

This was a shy one, despite his success in getting her body underneath his at the club. Shy, but with no aversion to PDA. An intoxicating contradiction.

Kirby had also been shy about saying what had happened with her ex-husband. But certain discussions were off-limits. Neither Liv nor Kirby's exes would be invited into his bedroom. Tonight, it was all about the two of them.

Make that the three of them.

"What's the puppy's name?" he asked as he turned the steak, which was almost ready.

Almost ready to burn if he didn't focus on the meal rather than those slits up the side of her dress.

"Baby," she said.

He couldn't help but smile. The song playing at the club? His slip in calling her *baby*? Could the name have anything to do with either, or was this another one of those coincidences that kept happening between them?

"Nice name. And since I know yours now, I won't call you *baby* anymore. I promise."

"Wise decision, especially with this one around," Kirby said, pointing to the puppy. "She already seems to know her name. If you say it, she might jump between us. I'm quite sure she's already in love with you."

*And I'm already in love with her*, Adam wanted to say. If only he were in a better position career-wise, he'd adopt Baby on the spot.

"Do your coworkers give their clients pet names in the throes of passion, too?" she asked.

There it was. The club. The token uninvited guest.

"Not to my knowledge."

Not entirely true. But he wasn't about to repeat some of the terms that had been bounced around.

Kirby must have been satisfied with that answer. As she walked away to examine the rest of his outdoor kitchen and patio, a cool breeze filled the space where she had stood. He found himself willing her back to his side.

He glanced over his shoulder.

She sipped from her wineglass and ran her hand along the back cushion of the all-weather sectional.

He couldn't wait a minute longer to take a tall sip of her. Even if it had to be a quick one.

With dinner under tentative control, he set down the spatula, walked over, eased the wineglass from her hand and set it on a table. He pressed into her, deep into that red dress, which would slip over her head quite easily. He then cupped her face in his hands and touched his lips to hers.

She opened herself to him, welcoming his tongue, which explored her even further. Her mouth felt as soft as red velvet cake, and tasted just as sweet. His length hardened as she reciprocated, teasing his tongue with hers. He pressed farther into her softness until he hit the spot that made her moan.

He could have devoured her right there, and it looked as if she would be willingly devoured. But Baby started barking.

The fish started burning.

The steak started flaming.

And all of his efforts to make a good impression went up in smoke.

"DAMN IT," ADAM SAID.

Kirby inwardly giggled. It was amazing he could move as fast as he did while sporting such a hard-on.

Otherwise, he seemed utterly deflated.

She steadied the tray while he halfheartedly transferred the charred remains of what would have been their dinner.

"I'm sorry, Kirby. I should have warned you this would happen. This always happens." He turned off the propane, put his hands on his hips and shook his head.

Time for ego-damage control, and she wouldn't even have to lie.

"Actually, I prefer my steak well done and my fish blackened." In fact, she always saved the burned edges for last.

She shifted the tray to one hand, then took his hand and led him back through the sliding glass door and closed it behind them, once Baby was safe inside.

After placing the feast on the counter, she opened drawer after drawer until she found the utensils. Plenty of spoons but no knives. Only one fork. Definitely workable.

She retrieved the fork, sliced into the charred fish and took a bite.

"Hot," she finally said as she fanned her mouth. "But soooooo good."

He eased the fork from her hand, grabbed a steak knife from a cutlery block nearby, sawed off a few bite-sized pieces of filet and popped a piece into his mouth.

"Not bad," he said.

She reclaimed the fork, carved off another piece of swordfish and held it up to his lips.

Adam opened his gorgeous mouth and allowed her to feed him. He slowly licked his lips and stared directly at her as if he were contemplating all the various ways to consume her. He continued their seductive dance by picking up a piece of the filet and holding it near her mouth.

As she received his offering, his fingers touched her lips, which fed a scorching flame straight to her lower belly as she imagined tasting him instead.

*My turn.* She picked up another piece of steak and fed it to him in the same way. Only, he slipped two of her fingers into his mouth along with the bite, and savored them before pulling away. Without pause, he leaned in and kissed her as if he were starving.

He moved forward, she moved back. Their lips never separated as he navigated them down a dark hallway, all the way to a bedroom. The reality of what was happening began to sink in as he lifted her dress so easily over her head.

"Do you mind if we turn down the lights?" she asked.

He scanned her almost-naked form and his gaze landed back on her face, focusing on her lips.

"Actually, I do. But, if it will make you more comfortable, I'll turn them down. This time."

After dimming the lights somewhat, he pulled off his T-shirt as he walked back toward her. The beauty of his chiseled pecs and abs set off an intoxicating pulse that traveled south from her heart to her core and lingered there.

He reached around and struggled with the hook on her bra as she tugged at the zipper on his pants. Their mutual struggle paid off. The bra slipped easily from her shoulders, with a little help from him. With a little help from her, his slacks soon pooled around his feet.

In a single, smooth motion, he removed his briefs, as well.

Her breath lodged in her throat. She'd already figured out he was well-endowed, but the beauty and strength of his erection caused her own sex to seize with anticipation.

They eased onto the bed, where he proceeded to peel down her panties, studying every inch of her along the way. He kissed his way back up, starting with her feet on up to her thighs, where he proceeded to part them.

*Definitely* not ready for that. She pressed her thighs back together and sat up.

"Please. I really want to," he said.

"No. Not yet."

She scooted farther back, and he eased on top, their bodies fitting together so effortlessly. So perfectly. He kissed her deeply, exploring her lips and mouth as she imagined him doing the exact same thing to her sex. She felt herself exploding, imploding at the thought of him wanting to do that to her. Begging.

*Please...*

He moaned as if he could feel her wetness increasing, but then he disconnected and pushed away. Fully away.

And her heart braced for the worst.

ADAM STUDIED THIS selectively timid, intoxicating contradiction of a woman in his bed. Half of him wanted to turn the lights completely up and study every single inch of her.

The other half was so turned on he couldn't reach into the bedside table drawer fast enough.

No, they hadn't discussed such a delicate issue, and he wasn't about to break the mood now. Even though they'd done little more than kiss, he was pretty sure she'd come already, which made it almost impossible for him not to. And someone who wanted the lights off might not be comfortable asking him to use protection.

He tore open the package and rolled the condom over his throbbing erection.

Her look of relief wasn't lost on him. And as soon as she voluntarily, albeit hesitantly, parted her legs to welcome him, nothing else seemed to matter.

Now *that* was an image he'd play over and over and over again.

He eased his full length into her slowly, when what he wanted to do was plunge as deep and fast and hard as possible. He managed to reel in that impulse when her body shuddered beneath him. Instead, he moved in even slower, deeper strokes.

She rewarded his decision with a soft, deep groan.

That did it. His mind zeroed in on the exquisite warmth wrapped around him.

Tight. She was so unbelievably tight. And hot. He'd never felt anything like her. No way he'd last long enough to give her a second orgasm, especially once he started kissing her again. She tasted of steak and wine, and he imagined how the rest of her would compare. In fact, he couldn't help but imagine he was kissing her hot velvet heat right now as he penetrated her in two places at once.

He explored her mouth. *Imagining, imagining...*until

the walls of her sex tightened fully around him. He could no longer hold back as he thrust as deep into her as possible.

She opened her eyes, and their gazes locked at the moment of his release. Then, with a soft, shy smile, she promptly looked away.

Although he could have stayed inside this heaven-on-earth forever, he reluctantly withdrew and laid beside her.

She promptly repositioned herself on her side, facing him, and rested one of her lovely arms across his chest.

Eventually, his breathing returned to some semblance of normal even though his heart kept beating out of his chest.

Either he'd forgotten how amazing a woman could feel, or he'd never had a good woman in his life, because she was unbelievable. And they didn't even get beyond missionary. He was definitely hungry for more of her.

Which reminded him. *Food.* His stomach growled at the thought.

"I heard that," she said.

Thankfully, she wasn't asleep.

Baby, however, was resting peacefully on one of the bed pillows they had managed to knock to the floor.

"I guess I'm still a little hungry. Especially since I missed out on dessert." Adam cleared his throat, then kissed the top of her head to let her know it was okay to be timid.

For now.

She looked at him, and damn if she wasn't more gorgeous with a postcoital glow.

At least, he assumed that was what happened, judging by the responsiveness of her body.

"Mine growled, too. I'm surprised you didn't hear it," she said.

"I could burn some asparagus for us."

"You can burn my asparagus any day."

Finally, a woman who appreciated his lack of culinary prowess.

"I do have something we can eat. Something I can't mess up," he said.

He eased out from under her embrace and stood, then promptly disposed of the condom in a nearby trash can for lack of a better immediate option.

Meanwhile, she sat up and arranged the sheet around her.

He peeled it away. "I've already seen you."

"Oh, really? With the lights turned down so low?"

"I guess I failed to mention my night vision." He grabbed the plaid wool blanket from the foot of the bed and spread it open.

"Here you go, oh, bashful one," he said.

She climbed out of bed, and he wrapped it around them both like a cocoon.

Together, they ambled down the hallway, all the way to the thick buffalo-hide rug in front of the fireplace.

He eased out from under the blanket.

"Sit," he commanded.

She complied.

"Stay," he continued.

Adam practically felt those gold-green eyes of hers looking over his completely nude body, which made his cock twitch again.

*Down, boy...*

He grabbed two spoons from the drawer and set them on the counter. Right next to the legal paperwork.

The stack represented an informal deposition mishmash of his prior problems, along with the newest allegation of theft. Oh, and his attorney's suggestion to file defamation charges against Donald Becker, so Adam had titled the document accordingly. Felt really good to list his name first.

He looked to Kirby, who had turned her attention back to the fire.

If timing was everything, he had everything in that moment. He opened the nearest drawer and stashed the document, then retrieved his second choice for dessert from the freezer.

He padded back to the fireplace, where his efforts earned him a fabulous lethal-weapon smile.

"The Häagen-Dazs!" she said as she opened the blanket for him.

He snuck a glance at her slender legs, which were folded to one side, and admired the way the warm glow of the lucky flames seemed to lick her skin. This time, however, she didn't shy away from being admired. Maybe he'd set a good example by acting so confident in the buff.

Maybe he'd continue to set a good example by turning up the lights next time. If there was a next time.

The realist in him admonished that he'd better enjoy all of this while he could. If he got a job in sunny Florida, there wouldn't be any need for a fireplace.

And, unfortunately, there wouldn't be any Kirby.

# 7

Kirby awoke to a glorious half-naked Adam leaning over, stoking some pitiful-looking embers.

It all came back to her, warm and easy. They'd come out to the great room, shared some ice cream and kisses in front of the fire and created a bed from blankets and pillows, and she must have fallen asleep.

He'd put on a pair of black sweatpants at some point but thankfully forgot the shirt.

Now that she was fully rested, every most-intimate inch of her reawakened with that hurts-so-good yearning over what they had done last night and what they might do next.

"May I help?" she asked.

He glanced down at her. "Good morning, beautiful. No, I've got it."

"Should we add some wood?" The idea of staying in front of the fire with him all day warmed her throughout, even though she had to get home to feed Lady at some point. Then again, Reese had a key, and she owed Kirby a favor.

"I better not start a fire I can't finish," he said.

The warm feeling cooled several degrees, and the "so-good" part of the hurts-so-good equation quickly diminished. Maybe she was getting a little too comfortable.

While he continued to stoke, Kirby wrapped herself in the blanket, slipped past him, grabbed her purse from the kitchen counter and wandered down the hall to the master bath. There, her pink toothbrush awaited, alongside some toothpaste.

Then it occurred to her. The paperwork she'd seen last night on the counter was missing. At least, it hadn't caught her eye when she had grabbed her purse. In fact, the island looked as if it had been wiped clean.

The whole thing served to remind her that, despite the physical intimacy, she still knew nothing about this man.

Reese was right. Kirby needed to be careful. Not to mention, she still needed to ask some questions. Pleasure kept getting in the way.

She brushed her teeth and washed her face. By the time she returned to the kitchen, he had his cell phone pressed against one ear and was deep in conversation.

Baby practically inhaled her breakfast from a bowl he had provided. For a fleeting moment, Kirby could totally see Baby as Adam's dog. They seemed to belong together, although she wouldn't dream of asking him to adopt her. Not with his work schedule being as nonstandard as hers.

He held up one finger to indicate he wouldn't be long.

Must not be too personal of a call, she concluded. He didn't move to another room, or even a few feet away.

"Now, what's this about again?" he asked the person on the other end. "Fine, but it better be important."

He slammed the phone on the counter.

"Is everything okay?"

"Lydia, my boss, called an emergency meeting for eleven."

"On a Sunday? Maybe those sofas started talking," Kirby said in the most playful tone she could muster.

No response from Adam as he poured some coffee for both of them.

"Hmm. I wonder what they would say. Perhaps something like, 'Enough already! You're wearing me out,'" she teased.

Adam looked at her but wasn't playing along. Instead, he grabbed both mugs and nodded toward the fireplace.

She settled into the sofa, accepted one of the coffees and took a sip.

After easing in beside her, he stole a quick and tender kiss. He set down his own mug and angled himself toward her, propping one elbow on the pillow behind him and resting his temple on his fist.

She recognized a serious-talk pose when she saw one. Of course, on him, the pose was seriously sexy. His flexing biceps and rippling abs competed against his baby blues for her attention.

"I'd like to get a few things out in the open. And, who knows, maybe you would, too. Especially since I'd like to see you again," he said.

She almost choked on her sip of coffee.

"Good idea."

What she wanted to say was that this was a risky idea. She hadn't prepared herself for any soul-baring discussions. She could hide her body beneath the blanket, but if he asked her what she did for a living, she'd have to come up with something that wasn't a complete lie.

Maybe she could tell him she was a rookie reporter, quietly excuse herself from The Deep assignment and take Seth's offer to cover the boring oil-and-gas scandal instead. No harm, no foul.

Except that would mean passing up another golden

opportunity, and for a man she barely knew. Even though the attraction was more intense than anything she'd ever felt, she'd be a fool to give up this chance for someone she'd known less than, what, seventy-two hours? Crazy. Besides, the jury was still out as to his own intentions.

"Look, Kirby, I don't want to be doing what I do at the club. I had some problems at my other job, and I landed at The Deep. I wanted to lay low until the problems faded and I could get on with my life. And…it looks as though that might happen soon. I'm up for a job in Florida."

*Florida?* His intentions seemed obvious now. To let her know he wasn't looking for anything remotely serious. Except for a serious job. But, hey, kudos for the honesty, even though it stung.

All the better, in a way. She'd tried to ignore her guilt over sleeping with him and still using him as a source. This slapped a titanium leash on those feelings. Then there was the other part of his confession…

"What kind of trouble, if you don't mind me asking?"

He ran his hand through his hair and expelled a nervous laugh.

"I can't believe I'm telling you this, but here goes. One of our equestrian clients accused me of harassment when I used to work as a trainer. None of it was true. But my employer believed her over me, although there wasn't any proof, and even less motivation on my part."

She studied his expression. Either he was telling her the truth, or he was the consummate liar.

"Okay. I believe you."

After all, he didn't have to reveal any of this to her. What would he have to gain? Yet, the information did raise more questions about him than it answered.

He rested his head back on the pillow as if the confession had taken so much out of him. "I can't tell you how much that was weighing on me."

"So, someone accused you of harassment. It's your word against hers. What I don't understand is why your employer wouldn't back your version."

"He might have, except some damn investigative reporter aired a story about it. My employer's other clients threatened to bail if he didn't terminate my contract. Because of the exposure. I was no longer employable in my field."

Something about the whole scenario nudged at her memory. It sounded vaguely familiar.

"Which reporter? He or she should be the one out of work."

"Seth Wainwright. A name and face I'll never forget. I haven't trusted a word that's come out of the news media's collective mouth since."

A chill crept across her flesh. Her instincts warned her to tread carefully.

"That's awful, Adam."

*In more ways than you know.*

He moved in close and hugged her tight. The chill dissipated beneath his warmth.

"Thanks for hearing me out, and for not bolting for the door."

No, she hadn't bolted. In fact, his admission gave her a segue to an unfortunate admission of her own. This was an opportunity to touch on the truth without cracking it wide-open, and to get his reaction.

"Since you brought up the topic, there's something I should probably tell you," she said. "I always wanted to be a reporter. But not the kind you described."

At that, he pulled away and gave her a questioning look.

"You're kidding, right?"

She shook her head. "My degree is in journalism. It would be nice to use it. In fact, it's my dream."

He exhaled a deep breath and looked away.

"So what's stopping you?" he asked without so much as glancing at her, as if he were addressing the flailing embers of the fireplace instead.

In fact, the dying embers offered a fitting metaphor for how their morning together was turning out.

"Just waiting for my big break. For now, I'm stuck behind a desk."

A partial truth, but at least she didn't lie. So much for testing waters. If she offered more, she'd likely alienate him *and* jeopardize the story.

"A desk job, huh? Nothing wrong with that." He finally looked at her with an obviously forced smile.

Not that she blamed him. She understood his hesitancy. If only there was a way she could make him understand her feelings, as well.

*Maybe there is.*

"I did have a chance, right out of college. A golden opportunity with a network affiliate."

"What happened?"

The wrong decision happened, impulsive and heated and driven by a desire over which she had no control. Rather, one that had complete control of her.

"I chose to follow a gold-plated opportunity instead. All the way from Chicago to Houston. Turned out the plating, and everything underneath, wasn't gold after all," she said, even though speaking the actual words almost made her choke.

He pulled her close and caressed her arm.

"What did he do to you, baby? You can tell me. You're safe here."

Maybe it was the way he called her *baby* again, but he made her feel safe. Even safe enough to confess what she'd needed to all along. What she'd been too humiliated to admit to family or friends, counselors or clergy.

Besides, if he rejected her after what she was about to say, then there wasn't a future between them anyway. Might as well find out now, and get an honest response rather than a paid-for one.

She swallowed hard, even though her mouth suddenly went dry and her lungs felt as though they were wrapped tight with the coarsest rope.

"My ex-husband didn't want me, sexually, after we got married. Couldn't bring himself to touch me in that way, and rejected me every time I tried to change his mind. Each rejection diminished me, as a woman, until I no longer felt like one at all."

Now she was the one who couldn't look him in the eye. But the door was open, and the painful truth needed an escape after being held in far too long.

"He wouldn't even kiss me. At least, not the way lovers kiss. He still loved me, so he claimed, but was simultaneously disgusted by me."

It was as if a long-festering wound had been lanced. She wanted to get all the sickness out of her system in a single purge.

She clenched her jaw and bit back the humiliation.

With a soft but firm hand, he angled her face toward his, and she reluctantly looked at him, fearful of what she would read in his expression.

Instead of repulsion, she saw bewilderment.

"Listen, that had nothing to do with you, Kirby. Some people pull that passive-aggressive bullshit to punish those they claim to love. Won't happen with me."

It wasn't what she had expected to hear, yet it was everything she needed.

"How can you be so sure? You don't even know me."

He shook his head.

"You're so beautiful, and you don't even realize how much. I'll make you a deal. I'll leave my baggage behind if you'll abandon yours."

"You've got a deal, baby." She initiated the kiss this time, and his body responded in full. It was as if Adam had reversed the guilty-of-being-undesirable verdict handed down by her ex.

Baby barked at their feet.

"She thinks we're talking to her. I better get dressed and take her for a walk," Kirby said.

Adam pulled her back down as she tried to stand.

"I'm already dressed. Sort of. I'll walk Baby. You get dressed, because I have to regrettably boot you out so I can get to the lame meeting on time."

Adam got up, leashed the puppy and left as if this was part of his normal morning routine.

After he and Baby were securely out the door and down the steps, she gulped the last of the coffee, took her empty mug to the kitchen and rinsed it out in the sink.

She also washed the spoon that he'd used to stir in the cream and sweetener, dried it with a hand towel and opened the utensil drawer.

There, on top of the spoons, sat the missing paper-work.

She lifted the first page, skimmed a little, then lifted the second page. Looked like a brief summary of the incident he had described. It even included the name of the accuser: Kelly, Madison.

She pressed a hand to her stomach. It felt as though

she'd been punched in the gut. Seeing the woman's name in print made it too real. Too personal.

All of a sudden, she couldn't be certain of how many minutes had passed and she sure didn't want him to catch her snooping. He'd been upfront about a life-changing accusation. She'd revealed her most devastating secret.

And neither one of them had bolted.

ADAM ESCORTED KIRBY to her car. She looked even better in that red dress in broad daylight.

Baby, however, had an agenda of her own. The puppy used Adam's legs as a shield as Kirby attempted to pick her up and put her into the car.

"Somebody doesn't want to leave," she said.

"Somebody doesn't want either of you to leave," he said. And he meant it.

Sort of. He had to get his head screwed on for today and tonight, and these two beauties were a serious distraction. But with his late hours, he wouldn't be home to feed and walk Baby, and it didn't feel right to invite Kirby to stay.

He still didn't know much about her, except that she wanted to be a reporter someday. Disappointing, yes. Liv had chased the spotlight and cheated in the shadows. Was a monogamous, drama-free relationship too much to ask for?

At the same time, he wanted Kirby to be happy. Truly wanted that for her. After all, she had been wounded in the worst way. No doubt about it.

He couldn't imagine ever withholding affection from someone he claimed to love, but he'd heard similar versions from his other customers. She had no reason to be embarrassed or ashamed. Hopefully, he had convinced her of that much.

She hugged him goodbye and drove away. He hadn't mentioned another date, but at least he'd talked about moving forward. That was, if he hadn't scared her off with his legal problems. Hell, he was the one who should be scared. That was exactly the information he shouldn't be talking about. With anyone.

His house was quiet until the phone rang. This was a call he'd better not ignore.

"Hey, Bernard."

"Hello, trespasser."

*Oh, yeah.* "Who told you?"

"Becker's attorney is a good friend of a friend. Big city, small world. Good news is, they aren't going to press charges."

"Good. They wouldn't have much of a case since I didn't steal the saddles."

"Oh, they're moving forward with that. They're not going to press charges for trespassing."

Adam massaged his temple. "For Christ's sake."

"Did you print out your notes like I asked? Or are you too busy getting into more trouble?"

"Yes and yes. I'll drop off a signed copy on my way to work."

He walked over to the drawer where he'd stashed the goods, but the drawer wasn't fully shut, as he'd left it.

Maybe he was being paranoid. Kirby and Baby had pretty much hijacked his brain and body last night. He was kind of surprised he'd managed to put the remainder of the ice cream back in the freezer.

"You there, Adam?"

"I'm here. I'll be at your office in less than an hour. I won't have time to chat about my newest indiscretions, so don't even bring them up."

"You're one indiscretion away from having to find a

new lawyer. Pull another stunt like the one you pulled yesterday, and I'm cutting you loose. You don't pay me enough for the grief."

"I don't pay you at all."

"Glad you admit it. So the least you can do is stay out of trouble."

"Oh, I plan to. Right after I finish my shift as a male prostitute."

"Very funny. Ride, is it? After we clear your name, you're getting out of there."

"If not sooner. But I'm not holding my breath. Don't hold yours, either." With that admonishment, he ended the call.

After all, Wild Indigo had yet to cough up an offer. In the meantime, only one thing could make his day less crappy.

With phone still in hand, he texted Kirby.

How about lunch? 1 p.m.?

I can't. Tomorrow? she texted back.

Want to see u 2-nite. Meet for a drink at 5?

Want to see u 2. I'll come to The Deep.

Definitely not.

Tomorrow then.

Can't wait that long. 5 at The Deep, it is. I'll book it.

Last thing he wanted was for her to come back to the club. Something told him he would regret it. But he'd regret not seeing her even more, and her best offer included the damn place. After what she confessed, he knew he shouldn't push too hard.

The next number he called belonged to Fabian.

"You better not be backing out of the meeting and expect me to tell Lydia," his friend said.

"No. I'm practically on my way now. As soon as I get dressed."

"Then what do you need? I'm in the middle of something, if you catch my drift."

No explanation required. The heavy breathing and deep moaning and squeaky box springs on the other end of the line said it all. Talk about multitasking.

"I guess you don't have a pen and paper handy," Adam said.

"Uh. If you want to wait a minute, I can get one."

"That would be rude to your date, man."

The female groans grew louder. The box springs practically screamed.

"Go ahead and tell me. I'll remember," Fabian said, somehow, in the middle of it all. "Just keep it short and sweet."

"Like your lovemaking technique? Okay then. Private room. Five o'clock," Adam said, even though he had no intention of breaking the cardinal rule at this point.

Well, maybe a few personal rules.

On the house.

# 8

By the time Kirby got situated at work, it was too late to dodge Seth. Thank goodness she'd be back at The Deep tonight. She wouldn't have to lie about that part when Seth asked. And he was about to ask. She could read it in his face.

Fortunately, an email from Bettencourt himself was parked in her inbox, cheering her on. It was the first personalized correspondence she'd ever received from the notoriously impersonal news director. Finally, she was being taken seriously here.

It also meant she better not screw this up, which she had come dangerously close to doing last night.

Seth rested one oversized butt cheek on the corner of her desk.

*Mental note: swab desk with disinfectant wipes.*

"Any progress?" he asked.

She nodded but offered nothing else.

His smile twitched ever so slightly.

"Spill it, Seth."

"You always can tell when I know something. What's your secret?"

"I don't give away my secrets."

She resumed scrolling through her emails, panning for more gold from Bettencourt. All the while, her peripheral vision kept tabs on Seth. She'd blossomed into something of an expert expression reader, and he practically flashed his proverbial hand despite his obvious efforts to play it close to the vest.

"Tell you what. You give me a hint at your secret, and I'll give you a hint as to what else I know about Easy Ride."

The possibilities of what he might know cut a swath through her, like a hot knife sinking into butter. Seth didn't do "nice," so whatever he was offering to kick up had to be dirt.

She was already confused enough, thanks to her onslaught of unexpected feelings for Adam. Any amount of unpalatable information would pretty much confirm her shaky judgment when it came to men.

All the more reason to hear it.

She stopped scrolling and gave Seth her full attention.

"Okay. I'll share. But you have to go first," she said.

"How do I know you'll keep your end of the bargain?"

"You hold the keys to the kingdom around here. Why would I try to pull anything over on you? Besides, I respect you far too much."

His defenses seemed to soften beneath flattery's warm glow.

*Bless his little weasel heart.*

"All right," he said. "Your gentleman friend's real name is Adam Drake."

He topped off the statement with a know-it-all smirk.

"Oh, please. I already know his name. Now I know you were the one snooping around on my computer. Why are you so infatuated by him? I'm pretty sure you're not his type."

"Very funny, Montgomery. And how convenient of you to already claim to know, now that I've stated it."

"It's true. You'll have to come up with something I don't know."

"Then you'll have to tell me what you *do* know."

"I know he hasn't always worked at The Deep. He had a more respectable career prior to his current job. How's that for a secret? Happy now?"

"Respectable? Is that what he said? You need to be very careful around this guy. He did something even less respectable in his past. Do the level of investigative work you're capable of and you'll find out the rest."

With that, he finally shimmied his way off the edge of her desk.

"How convenient to tell me absolutely nothing of value," she said. "I know about the allegations of harassment levied against him. I even know the name of the accuser. Keep talking."

"Now that's an interesting twist, since the name of the accuser was never released."

Seth half pursed his lips in anticipation of her reaction. Either he knew the name, or he was baiting her for something else.

"I'm sorry you don't believe me," she said. "But you have to know the name of the accuser. You did the investigation."

"Yes, I did. I investigated a claim of sexual impropriety against Adam Drake. The name of the accuser wasn't released because she was a minor."

ADAM HAD NEVER been to Deep in the Heart on a Sunday morning. The place looked so lifeless without the crowds of people. Like a cavernous lung, complete with high wood-beam ceilings as its rib cage. It needed people and music and dancing in order to breathe.

Sunday night, however, the place practically hyperventilated, as if all the sinners felt depleted after confessing their sins at church, and returned in the evening to replenish.

The dance floor reminded him of Kirby and the night they met. Sure, he had suspected she was his client, with the way she clutched the ticket and had that panicked first-timer look about her as the ticket slipped from her hands. As fate would have it, Lydia had sent him out into the club to find Gentleman John. Instead, he found Kirby.

He reached the red door and plugged in his code.

The other guys had already arrived. Their expressions ranged from bored to perplexed. Lydia obviously hadn't offered any hints regarding the nature of this mandatory meeting. Fabian's messed-up hair and wrinkled T-shirt confirmed what Adam already knew. The guy had just rolled out of bed, sleep-deprived but fully satisfied in other ways.

Adam felt satisfied, too, for the first time in a long time. It felt damn good. But the similarity between him and his best friend ended there.

"Where's Lydia?" Adam cast out his query to the group.

"She's on her way. Traffic jam," Fabian said.

"Any idea what this is about?" Adam asked.

A few of the guys shrugged.

Lydia finally arrived with her hair arranged in her trademark messy bun, which triggered thoughts of Kirby all over again.

"I'm sure y'all are wondering why you're here," she said.

Most of the guys offered less-than-enthusiastic nods.

"To begin, I got a complaint from the cleaning crew. Do not make me repeat what they claim to have found on the Corbusier in room two."

Adam's stomach pitched.

Cowboy Roy snorted.

"I figured it was you," Lydia said. "Next time, please use a condom. Which brings me to item number two. Condom disposal. The cleaning crew also brought it to my attention that one of the toilets was clogged and requires a major repair. Anyone want to fess up? Who here wears a Trojan Magnum XL and went through more than one last night?"

*Seriously?* Were they really having this discussion? And did the cleaning crew really inspect the violation thoroughly enough to determine the brand and size of the offender?

Gentleman John sat up straight and raised his hand, as if he got bonus points for being freakishly endowed. He seemed pleased with himself until Lydia explained how the repair costs would be deducted from his earnings.

Nothing like the threat of a reduced paycheck to shrink a guy back down to normal size.

The whole thing felt surreal, and as casual as their discussions on what music they should pipe in, if any. Or whether the light fixture in the entry should be a contemporary Euro design or a 1930s-era Czechoslovakian crystal flush-mount chandelier.

"What should we do with 'em?" Cowboy Roy asked.

Lydia massaged her temples. "How about you stick to the house rule. Save that kind of activity for outside the club. Which brings me to point number three. Save that kind of activity for outside the club."

This time, most of the guys snickered.

Lydia usually remained pretty cool, but Adam could tell she was starting to lose it. Her tight skin stretched further, and her face turned a medically dangerous shade of crimson.

"Okay, boys. Have it your way, while you can. I wasn't going to mention this until I knew more, but apparently some female reporter is more than a little curious about the type of services we provide here. I don't think I have to spell out what negative publicity could mean for us."

"Is the reporter hot?" one of the guys asked.

Lydia didn't dignify it with an answer. She simply shook her head and stormed out of the room. As soon as the clicking of her stilettos had faded, some of the guiltier parties burst out laughing.

She didn't have to spell it out for Adam. If Lydia's suspicions were true, and if the goings-on inside the club were made public, he'd be screwed.

*SEXUAL IMPROPRIETY? With a minor?*

It felt as though the air had been suctioned out of her lungs.

Kirby had refused to show that she was flustered. Not in front of Seth, of all people. No doubt he'd still read something into the fact that she'd excused herself to the ladies' room, practically tripping over her own boots to get there.

She gripped the toilet seat and willed herself to heave. Nothing.

In fact, she hadn't eaten anything today. This latest disgusting news filled the void instead. Images of nubile sixteen-year-olds flashed before her eyes as she made her way back to the computer.

No wonder Adam hadn't gone into much detail about

the allegations. And she'd skimmed the document too quickly to pick up on it.

Thank God she hadn't fully confessed about her job. Or, worse, allowed her libido to abandon The Deep and take Seth up on his offer to trade.

Once back at her desk, she texted Adam. She wouldn't make it to the club tonight, as much as she could use some decent video footage and a confession or two for what she should have stayed focused on in the first goddamn place. No alternate plan, no explanation, no embellishment offered. She didn't shut the door completely—no way she intended to drop the story—but she closed it enough to keep him out while she followed this unfortunate lead.

She logged back into her computer and typed in a name she had committed to memory. Kelly Madison. The search engine offered its findings. All seventeen gazillion of them, including several Facebook links.

She spent most of her time ruling out the obvious leads, leaving her with nothing of substance.

An hour later, the hungry ache in her stomach refused to be ignored. She plodded over to the vending machine, slipped in some quarters and pressed the three-digit number that would reward her with a much-needed bag of peanuts.

The machine unspooled a package of Flamin' Pork Rinds instead.

Of course. She'd transposed the numbers.

The irony struck her with a vengeance. She practically ran back to her computer and typed in the transposed version of the name she'd memorized.

Like a stroke of atypically good luck, the first page of results offered a Madison Kelly in Houston, Texas, listed under Kelly Farms. When she clicked on the site,

Madison's name popped up beneath the name and photo of Todd Kelly, owner and trainer.

The website listed Madison as an employee. No photo.

Kirby's imagination proceeded to draw one anyway. A very young, pretty one.

According to the site, Kelly Farms didn't train on Sundays, but their office was open.

She picked up the receiver and punched in the number. She didn't have a script in mind, but since she was looking to find out the truth, that's how she would start.

"Kelly Farms. Todd speaking."

"Hi there. I'm trying to reach Madison Kelly. Is she working today?"

"You wanna talk to Madison?"

*Not really.*

"Yes. Is this her brother?"

"Yes, ma'am. Who are you, and what is it you need? Not to sound rude, but no one ever asks for Madison."

"I'm Kirby Montgomery. Channel 53. I need to ask her a few questions, off the record."

A deep sigh flooded the phone line.

"Oh, boy. What did she do now?"

AFTER THE MEETING with Lydia and the guys, Adam felt like going straight home and taking a hot shower. Yeah, he'd known what was going on, but he hadn't realized the extent of it.

He had a full night of clients to face. Could one of them be the alleged reporter? He was grateful for having a modicum of sexual self-restraint when it came to work.

He hadn't welcomed Kirby's confession regarding her career ambitions, but now it felt downright intrusive. He took some comfort in assuming she wouldn't have mentioned it if she were working on a story about the club. Maybe he could chalk this up to yet another coincidence.

Besides, he'd been looking forward to seeing her since the moment she'd driven away. Problem was, they'd already arranged to meet at the club, and he couldn't let that happen. Especially now.

Fabian headed his way, acting none too surprised about anything they'd heard.

"Really? Someone left a deposit on a sofa?" Adam asked as soon as Fabian was within earshot.

"Apparently. That's disgusting, even by my standards. Then there's the other issue."

"How much do we know?"

"Not much. One of Gentleman John's clients mentioned that an investigative reporter had asked her some questions about this place. Hopefully, that's as far as it went."

"What did his client tell the reporter?"

"That, I don't know. But I do know that this particular client has it bad for John. She even told him she loved him, if you can believe it."

"Eye of the beholder," Adam said.

"Damn straight. My theory is, she probably wants to scare him into behaving with his other customers. Otherwise, she would have provided more information, don't you think? I'm not overly concerned. And you sure as hell haven't done anything to be worried about."

Fabian's confidence eased some of Adam's suspicions as they headed toward the entrance.

"Any chance all my appointments canceled?"

"I'll check, but I doubt it." Fabian eased behind the podium and tapped into the iPad while Adam pulled his cell phone from his pocket.

A text from Kirby.

"Looks like I got one cancellation," Adam said. "Kirby won't be stopping by at five."

He felt simultaneously disappointed and thoroughly relieved. If she were the reporter, and had a chance to get back into the club, she wouldn't be backing out.

On a more personal level, he tried not to read too much in to her minimalist wording. Still, something felt wrong. If she'd put a smiley-face emoji at the end of her message, he'd know she hadn't changed her mind about seeing him altogether.

"That's news. I didn't know she was your five o'clock private," Fabian said.

"Yes, but not for the reasons you're thinking." No way he'd do anything inside the club with Kirby or anyone else, tainted Corbusier notwithstanding.

"Why didn't you say it was for her?" Fabian asked.

"You were busy tearing up the sheets when I called. And I guess I forgot to mention it in all the excitement about the clogged toilet. But, hey, I learned something new. You shouldn't flush condoms."

"And that Gentleman John wears an extralarge. No wonder the ladies fall heels over head in love with him." Fabian punctuated the statement with a snort.

"Can we change the subject? I'm a very visual person."

"Right after I answer your original question. You have one other cancellation. Your ten o'clock."

Ten. He would love to ask Kirby if he could stop by her place, but ten o'clock sounded too much like a booty-call time slot.

No, he'd try her in a while, get the scoop on the meaning behind the text and maybe plan a real date. Complete with dinner and dancing and all the schamltzy stuff his grandfather admonished him to do, when all Adam really wanted was to nestle himself between those luscious thighs of hers, and dive into her soft, hot, wet—

"Wanna pump some iron?" Fabian said, interrupting the stimulating visual Adam had going. "We've got plenty of time before work."

"I would, but I need to stop by the hospital. They're releasing Henry, and I'm driving him home."

"Now, see, there's some good news."

Definitely good. He simply hoped his grandfather didn't ask him anything more about the Florida gig.

Still, no news was better than bad news when it came to his job. Or the club, for that matter. Especially when it was the kind of news that would be delivered straight from some reporter's mouth.

# 9

Kirby stood at the threshold of Kelly Farms, at Todd Kelly's invitation. She wasn't so sure she wanted to see this woman-child who had accused Adam of such a terrible thing. Yet, this was one threshold she needed to cross to get to the truth.

Madison's own brother had admitted that his little sister possessed quite a propensity for telling lies of all shapes and sizes, without compunction. That she had more emotional problems than one little girl should have to shoulder, and that he'd done what he thought necessary to protect her. Now, he insisted Kirby hear Madison's admission for herself.

"Straight from the horse's mouth," he had said over the phone. "Let's get this out in the open, undo the damage to that young man's reputation if we possibly can, and give everyone's wounds a fighting chance to heal."

She knocked on the only front door she could find and was greeted by a nice-looking young man clad in a flannel button-down, faded working jeans and cowboy boots. Clint Eastwood, circa 1956, but without the celebrity shine.

"Come on in, Ms. Montgomery. Have a seat." He

pointed to a hickory ladder-back chair facing a matching desk.

The place smelled of tobacco and burned coffee and saddles.

He eased into the distressed leather executive chair on the other side, picked up the phone receiver and punched in some numbers.

"Madison. Come see me in the office, sweetheart. What? Yes, she's here."

He hung up the phone and exhaled a long sigh. "She doesn't like to meet new people. And I'm sorry to make you come all this way. Your coworker never responded to my phone calls, some ten months ago. I guess they finally passed the message along to you."

Kirby blinked. "You tried to call our station?"

"Yep. I called that Seth Wainwright character directly. Twice. Got his voice mail both times. He never returned my call."

That explained a lot. If presented with a retraction from the accuser, Seth would have to admit he was wrong in airing the story and endure the subsequent hand slap. So he sacrificed Adam's career and reputation by letting his initial report stand. No wonder Adam didn't care for reporters.

Just as she started to regret how she'd canceled on him, a soft knock on the door jolted her from her thoughts.

A young, gangly teenager with glasses and braces and long, stringy blond hair entered the room but parked herself near the door.

"Madison, this is Ms. Montgomery."

Kirby held out her hand for the girl to shake, but Madison stared at her own feet instead.

"Madison, I want you to tell this nice lady what happened at Becker Farms last year between you and Mr. Drake."

"I don't know what you're talkin' about," Madison said without looking up.

"It's okay, sweetheart," Todd said. "You aren't being punished. We talked about this less than an hour ago, remember? We gotta make it right, and Ms. Montgomery might be able to help us do that."

Madison seemed to consider his words while Kirby held her breath.

"Nothin' happened. Mr. Drake never did nothin' to me," Madison finally offered. She made the briefest possible eye contact.

"What did you accuse him of, if I may ask?" Kirby said.

The girl shuffled from one foot to the other and bit her bottom lip.

"Go on. Answer her," Todd said.

"I said he touched me. Here." She pointed in the general area of her breasts.

"Were the police involved?" Kirby asked, directing her question to Todd.

"Initially, yes. To make it worse, one of the parents got wind of it and called your station. But then Madison got spooked after seeing the report. Wouldn't cooperate and kept changing her story, so charges were eventually dropped. A couple months later, she told me she'd made it up. I could tell she felt awful about it."

"Did you contact Becker Farms to tell them what you knew?"

Todd looked down and shook his head.

"I thought long and hard about it, believe me. But Madison needed help real bad with some other issues she was havin', and I didn't want to put her through anything else. I did try contacting Adam Drake, but he'd disconnected his number and pretty much disappeared. So I decided to let sleepin' dogs lie. Then you called."

"Why did you make up a story, Madison?" Kirby asked.

"I don't know. I thought he liked me, but then he started dating some older girl. A really pretty one. Even got her stupid name tattooed on his arm."

Kirby winced. She had noticed something odd within the ink on his bicep.

"So, your feelings were hurt, and you wanted to hurt him back," Kirby said.

Madison looked down again. "I s'pose."

Kirby glanced at Todd, who shrugged.

"You can go now, Madison," he said.

"Thank you for confiding in me," Kirby said as the girl made a hasty exit.

Not only did this confirm what she wanted so desperately to believe about Adam, but it also proved that Seth was a weasel.

And there was nothing like the truth to put a weasel in his place.

By the time Adam arrived at the hospital, Henry was partially dressed and sitting up in bed.

"Sorry I'm late," he said without explanation.

"You're right on time. You don't need to coddle me. These pretty nurses can handle it." Henry winked at the one who was taking his blood pressure one final time.

"The release papers have been signed," the nurse said. "I'll be back in a few minutes."

Adam helped Henry put on his shoes.

"How did your date go last night?" Henry asked.

"It went well. I cooked dinner for her. Hey…how did you know I had a date? I don't recall telling you."

"I figured it out, like I figured out you had a crush. And…?"

"And nothing. This is brand-new. It could go either way," Adam said as he helped Henry with his jacket.

"How did you meet your future wife?"

Adam shook his head. "You don't give up, do you?"

"I'm still here after passing out and landing facedown in my yard, according to a jury of my peers. Obviously I'm not going anywhere. Except Destin," Henry said, with two thumbs up.

*Florida.* He knew how excited Henry was about moving, but he still couldn't give him an official reason to be.

He chose his next words carefully. "We met in the grocery store."

"I hope you weren't wearing those sweats at the time."

Of course his grandfather would say that. He was of the generation when courting was an art form.

"She was wearing yoga pants. We sort of matched. I saw it as a sign."

"A sign indeed. Grocery stores are magical places," Henry said.

"I'm inclined to believe you."

Adam walked to the sink and collected Henry's toothbrush and toothpaste and put them in a small travel bag he'd retrieved from his grandfather's house on the way over.

He smiled inwardly at the grocery-store coincidence and, for a moment, he considered telling his grandfather about the toothbrush proposal. But such an admission would lead to other questions he didn't care to answer.

"Did you reach for the same head of iceberg, by chance?" Henry asked.

"Not exactly. We met over prewashed packaged lettuce. Hearts of Romaine, of all things."

"Oh, you young folks and your conveniences. It isn't iceberg, but the name itself is a good sign. Yep, a good sign indeed."

Fortunately, the doctor interrupted, followed by a nurse pushing a wheelchair.

"Come see me at the office next week. We'll check your blood work," the doctor said.

"I'm sure I'll be fine. I can walk out of here. No need to bother the nurse with the wheelchair."

"Sorry," the doctor said. "Hospital rules."

Henry reluctantly agreed, but only after offering the nurse a conspiratorial wink.

Ordinarily, Henry would have played matchmaker at this point. The odd detour from his usual modus operandi meant only one thing. It was apparent, even to his grandfather, that Adam wasn't entirely available.

On the one hand, he was glad he could give Henry a glimmer of hope. On the other, it was yet another way he might let the man down.

Who was he fooling? The wording of Kirby's text continued to chafe. It felt like a blow-off, and she'd yet to return his call.

She never did offer her address. Maybe she really was like some of the women who came into the club for sexual validation only. In Kirby's case, she got what she needed. And she didn't even have to pay for it.

BECKER FARMS WASN'T a farm at all. It was an entire equestrian center, complete with indoor and outdoor arenas and turnout areas, and a scrolled iron security gate protecting it all. In the distance, riders practiced drills in two separate open arenas.

Kirby could totally picture Adam here. She could also picture how a young, impressionable girl could develop a huge crush on him.

She located a keypad and intercom near the gate and followed the instructions. Once again, she didn't have a script in mind. All she knew was she had to talk to somebody in charge about Adam.

"Yes? May I help you?" a woman's voice asked.

"I hope so. My name is Kirby Montgomery. I'm with Channel 53 news. I don't have an appointment, but— "

A loud buzz was followed by the opening of the main gate.

*Someone actually welcomes the press?*

*That someone might not welcome me for long.*

She drove down a long trail toward a compound of assorted buildings and parked in front of what looked to be the main one.

A woman stepped outside and met her halfway.

"I'm Trish Becker. My husband isn't here right now. Are you investigating the missing saddles?"

*The what?* "Actually, I'm here to talk to you about Adam Drake and the allegations of sexual misconduct."

Trish glanced around as if making sure no one could overhear them.

"You should probably wait until Donald gets back. I wasn't involved in that whole incident."

"But you know what happened?" Kirby asked.

Trish hesitated.

"This is completely off the record," Kirby said. "I'm simply doing some research for my own benefit."

"Come inside," Trish said, leading the way.

Yep. This place was much fancier than Kelly Farms, even though the other was quite charming. And thoroughly Western.

This one screamed English saddle, dressage, with Western pleasures tucked away in the far corner. It brought to mind something she'd noticed at Adam's house—how accoutrements such as bridles and helmets sat in the corner nearest the back patio door. A couple of saddles, as well.

Instead of sitting behind the desk, Trish invited Kirby to get comfortable on an oversized cream-colored leather sectional, and then settled in beside her.

Kirby angled herself toward the woman so she could hopefully read her expressions.

"I'll get right to the point, Mrs. Becker. I spoke with Madison Kelly, and she recanted her allegations against Adam Drake. Off the record, for now, but I wanted you and your husband to know the truth about that whole incident, in case it makes a difference about anything."

"You spoke to Madison? In person?"

"Yes, ma'am. I just came from Kelly Farms."

Trish shook her head. "I always thought she had made up the story. But why? And why wouldn't Todd let us know?"

"I think it boils down to a misguided attempt to protect his sister from any further embarrassment. She's apparently quite fragile, mentally and emotionally. From what she told me herself, she had a crush on Adam but he started dating someone else instead, which prompted the accusation."

"I guess I can't blame her for being infatuated with him. But to take it so far? And then the reporter aired the whole thing as if it were true?"

*That's our Seth*, Kirby wanted to say. Instead, she allowed Trish to continue.

"We had no choice but to let Adam go. Our other customers insisted upon it. They didn't want him near their daughters. Even though the whole topic seemed to disappear as quickly as it appeared, the televised report left a permanent stain."

"You mentioned something about some missing saddles," Kirby said.

"Yes. Hermès. Donald takes inventory once a year, and discovered two of them missing. Unfortunately, the last time he took inventory was right before he dismissed Adam."

"He thinks Adam took them?"

"He was the only other person with a key. I know my husband doesn't believe it in his heart, but there's no other explanation."

"Would such expensive saddles have serial numbers?" Perhaps she could somehow cross-check them against the ones at Adam's house, although his saddles didn't appear to be designer.

"Of course," Trish said.

"Could I have a copy of those? I'd like to look into this further, and I can let you know what I find out. If anything."

Trish walked over to a filing cabinet, looked through some folders and pulled out a list.

"I'll make a copy for you and highlight the missing ones," Trish said, then disappeared into the next room.

While she was gone, Kirby studied the photos on the wall. Adam stood proud next to riders on their decorated horses, or with students in the arena. Other trainers and clients were pictured, as well. Dozens of photos not only filled one wall, but the frames also spilled over to the next one. He looked the same in some ways, yet different. Younger. Leaner. Shorter hair. But still a total knockout.

Even though this place had expelled Adam as a

trainer, they hadn't bothered to take down his picture, which struck her as odd.

Obviously, they still respected him, which on some level meant they still trusted him.

Another thing that stood out: no photos of Madison on the wall. She'd obviously been a short-timer and must have quit soon after the Beckers dismissed Adam. If he were no longer there, why wouldn't have she continued on? Unless she had something else to hide. This whole chain of reasoning spawned another theory about the missing saddles.

Trish returned, papers in hand.

"Nice photos. Adam is very handsome," Kirby said.

"He was our best trainer, you know. And he's as polite as he is handsome."

"I know," Kirby said.

Trish cocked her head. "You've met him? Well, I suppose you did say you'd come here for personal reasons."

Maybe she shouldn't have said anything. In retrospect, she shouldn't have used her real name, either, or stated her affiliation with the media, in case Trish or her husband decided to contact Adam.

"Yes, we've met," Kirby said. "If you talk to him, I hope you won't mention I was here. He'd never forgive my snooping around, but I'd like to see this resolved. For Adam's sake."

"I understand. But I'll definitely tell Donald about Madison's confession. Not that it will make a difference until this mystery with the saddles is solved."

If Kirby's new hunch regarding the missing saddles was correct, she'd gladly share that information with Trish, as well. On the other hand, if her hunch was wrong and Mr. Becker was right, she'd never trust her instincts, or Adam, again.

# 10

"I DON'T UNDERSTAND. Why would he cheat? Am I really so horrible?"

Adam's client rested her head on his shoulder. He resisted the urge to scoot away. Instead, he rubbed her arm and counted down the remaining minutes.

"You deserve better. I think you know that," he said.

Although it was a stock line, it probably applied in most cases. It also hit home. Liv had cheated. Was he really so horrible? Furthermore, was Kirby seeing someone else? Was that the message buried between the lines of her vague and noncommittal and not-the-tiniest-bit-encouraging text?

More than ever, he felt stuck in this vortex of having to soothe strangers' emotions, sort out his own, protect Henry's and decode Kirby's.

At least the woman didn't try to kiss him. He'd been dodging kisses from customers since he first kissed Kirby, as if he'd been gladly branded. Like a bull, which was rather fitting, considering this place.

"Go home, take a warm bath and get some rest," he said as he proceeded to stand. His customer sure wasn't taking the initiative.

The woman nodded as if he'd prescribed something of value.

His stock line actually sounded damn good at the moment. He should take his own advice and go home, rather than do something stupid such as call Kirby again. But, if this relationship were the Kentucky Derby, Stupid would be leading Common Sense by a furlong.

He escorted his client to the exit but didn't go outside. He'd only done that with Kirby. Instead, he headed to the foyer to do something even more idiotic.

"Congratulations, my friend. You're done for the evening," Fabian said as he tapped at the iPad in front of him.

"Not quite, Fab."

"Oh, yeah? Did your girlfriend take the ten o'clock without booking through appropriate channels?"

"No. I'm going to her house."

"Well, this is moving right along. I mean, I definitely see the attraction, but isn't she on the rebound?'"

The possibility had all but eluded Adam. Now it slammed into him with full force. A rebound situation would explain why she'd backed off.

"Probably," Adam said. "Which is why I need to see her tonight. But I need your help."

Fabian shook his head. "Oh, no. Not doing it. Not even for my best friend. If the two of you were so close, she would have given you her address."

"Come on, Fab. I'm not a stalker and you know it. I want to check on her. Make sure she's okay."

"That's what phones are for, Ride. Call or text her."

"She isn't returning my calls or texts."

"Then take a *hint*."

Even for Fabian, that was particularly cruel. It was also particularly logical.

"Her address. Nothing more. I won't tell a soul."

*And Stupid wins by a furlong.*

Fabian seemed to consider, then shook his head with more conviction. "I can't do it. I need this job. No one else will hire me."

Adam exhaled. "You're probably right."

Truth was, Adam did understand. As much as he wanted to see Kirby tonight, he didn't want to jeopardize his friend's job. Even if the friend was being a major asshole.

"I've got to run to the men's room," Fabian said. "Will you man my post for a few minutes?"

Adam massaged his temples. "Yeah. Sure. Even though you refuse to help me, I'll help you. Jeez."

"Pocket the attitude." Fabian pointed at the designated spot behind the podium and disappeared beyond the scrim.

Adam reluctantly assumed the appropriate place and checked the iPad to see if any clients were likely to show up in Fabian's absence.

There, on the screen, was Kirby's entire confidential dossier.

Address and all.

ADAM LOOKED UP at the Elysian Lofts in midtown, trying to guesstimate which window on the third level would be hers.

He really had turned into a stalker, and not even a good one. Although the Stetson had seemed like a good idea, Houston proper wasn't anything like his little slice of the pie outside the city, or inside Deep in the Heart.

He removed the hat and summoned the nerve to slip past someone who had exited the locked front entrance.

Inside, the concierge flirted with one of the guests or perhaps one of the residents.

Adam took advantage of the distraction and walked right by as if he knew where the hell he was going. He followed the unmistakable *ping* of the elevators and slipped inside. So much for security.

The third-floor hallway was as poorly marked as the lobby. No directional plaques anywhere. He looked to the left and then to the right, and chose the right.

*Wrong.*

He tiptoed back in the other direction. Yet, his boots still slapped against the polished concrete hallway. Yep. He made for a lousy stalker in his Luccheses.

Just his luck, Unit 332 happened to be at the far end of a long hall. Instead of knocking, he stood outside the door for a reflective moment. What if she weren't alone? What if she got royally pissed off over him showing up unannounced when she hadn't even given out her address?

*What if you knock on the damn door and find out?*

After a few more moments of worthless contemplation, he gave in to his inner voice.

The frantic barks of that crazy-faced, floppy-eared puppy were unmistakable. Baby was going berserk on the other side. Had the puppy somehow recognized his knock?

He didn't hear Kirby's footsteps, but the door swung open and there she stood. Barefoot and beautiful. And wrapped in a cozy white blanket.

The look propelled his thoughts back to the two of them wrapped together in a thick blanket, walking down the hall from his bedroom to the great room and settling in for the night in front of the fireplace.

"Hello. How, exactly, did you find out where I live? I'm pretty sure I didn't tell you," she said.

"You talk in your sleep," he lied.

She squinted. "I do not. Do I?"

He simply nodded. No way he'd disclose his source. He owed Fabian that much.

"I warned you I'm not the type of stalker to hide behind lettuce displays. I wanted to make sure you're okay. Are you?" he asked.

Instead of slamming the door in his face, she eased into his arms.

"I'll take that as a 'yes,'" he said.

Her blanket dropped to the ground. She felt like pure satin in his embrace.

No wonder. She stood drenched in an apricot-colored satin tank top and matching pajama bottoms.

Immediately, his brain calculated the most efficient way to remove each of the items.

She picked up her blanket, pulled him inside and closed the door behind them.

"I'm so sorry I didn't return your call or text. My head's been pretty messed up lately." Her words were chased by what sounded like an ironic laugh.

Yep. Coming here wasn't his brightest idea.

"Not because of me, I hope."

She seemed to think about it for a moment, then shook her gorgeous head.

"No. Of course not. I got a terrible migraine. So I came home, took a long bath and tried to sleep."

Her hair was beautifully disheveled, as if she'd been lying on a beach somewhere, the wind tousling her long brown strands.

Or, the same way she had looked in front of his fireplace after their night of sex.

As before, she wore very little makeup. Yet her dark brows, thick lashes and pink lips didn't need any embellishment. She looked sexy as hell in a just-rolled-out-of-bed sort of way.

"Can I get you anything? A soda? Some ice cream?" he asked.

She wrapped the blanket tight around herself.

"No, thanks. Migraines make me nauseated and my stomach is finally getting back to normal. Don't want to push it. I'm sorry about my text. I wasn't myself."

"No apology necessary. Sit down. Let me burn you a bowl of soup or something," he said.

"You don't have to—"

"I know. I have an ulterior motive for doing it, so don't feel guilty about accepting."

He ventured into the kitchen area, taking in his surroundings along the way. Multitone brick walls, exposed piping overhead on the tall ceilings, plenty of windows but no greenery beyond them. Only the face of other buildings and the street below.

Felt a bit like a prison. Although he wouldn't mind being locked up in here with her.

"Okay. I found a saucepan. Where's your soup?" he asked.

"Cabinet on the far left. If there's even any in there."

She wasn't kidding. Only one can. If broth even qualified as soup.

He fished around in the drawers and located a manual can opener. A few minutes on medium-high heat and… "Voilà! Dinner is served."

Chicken broth, heated to perfection. No burned edges.

He poured some of the murky liquid in a mug and joined Kirby on the sofa.

She took a sip and licked her lips. It took all his will-power to not lean over and steal a kiss.

"So, what else did I say in my sleep?" She raised the mug to her lips, her eyes never deviating from his.

Talk about an opportunity.

"You described all the things you want to do with me. All the things you're going to let me do to you."

She nearly choked on a sip.

That confirmed it. She'd at least thought about a few things. Maybe the same few things he'd imagined.

"I think I see what's happening," she said. "This is a booty call."

He eased the cup from her hand and tasted the brew. Not bad.

Not much of a dinner, but he wasn't about to offer to cook anything more complicated. He'd burn something for sure, because the apricot satin that clung to certain curves of her body was simply too distracting for words. In fact, he wouldn't mind another glimpse.

"I'd never use you for a booty call. Especially when you're not feeling well. But I'm still getting more than a little turned on. Is that wrong?"

He rubbed his hand along her back and shoulders, then tugged at the blanket, revealing the satin loveli-ness of her pajama top.

She set down her cup, leaned into him and buried her face in the crook of his neck.

Not quite the move he hoped for, but a good start.

He put an arm around her and caressed her. Unlike with the customer earlier, he wanted to pull Kirby even closer.

"How was your day, or do I want to know?" she asked.

"It started out really good. I woke up in front of my fireplace, next to this gorgeous woman."

"Really? And it went downhill from there?"

"Straight to the bowels of hell."

"Did it have anything to do with your meeting?"

"As a matter of fact, it did."

"Anything I should know about. As a client?"

The *c* word felt like a kick to the gut.

"About that. I'm ending the working part of our relationship, effective immediately. Apparently, things are happening at the club that I can't even repeat."

"Let me guess. The guys are sleeping with their clients."

He neither confirmed nor denied. He was too busy kicking himself for even bringing it up, especially after the bombshell Lydia dropped at the meeting. Make that multiple bombs. She'd given new meaning to "shock and awe."

"Your refusal to answer could be interpreted as an admission. Care to set the record straight?" Kirby asked.

The timing of her questions couldn't have been worse. It rubbed him the wrong way, and just when everything else about her was rubbing him the right way.

Like the way she planted a tender, slow-motion kiss on his lips.

"Wouldn't you rather know how a certain beautiful woman's refusal to return my call or texts affected me?" he said.

"Can you ever forgive her?"

Adam kissed the top of her head. "Maybe. If she's willing to convince me that she wants to see me now."

Kirby bit her luscious bottom lip. "And how might she accomplish such a thing?"

Adam slipped the blanket from the rest of her body,

then eased her on top of him until she was sitting on his lap, facing him.

Straddling him.

His erection began to strain against his jeans as she took the lead in kissing him while unbuttoning his shirt.

He rested his hands on her hips as she moved tentatively.

The satin glided easily against him.

He took control of her movement and guided her back and forth, more firmly. As her beautiful eyes closed, her moan indicated he'd hit the magic spot. He focused on that spot, daring to dream how it would feel and taste against his lips, his tongue.

As the thought consumed him, he threw his head back. "What are you doing to me?"

She planted a soft, warm kiss on the side of his exposed neck, and it delivered an electric jolt to his already energized loins.

"I'm trying to convince you. Are you convinced?" she said.

"I'm getting close."

"Maybe this will help." She eased the silk top over her head.

It nearly put him over the edge to see her soft breasts in so much light. Damn, she was perfect.

As she continued her easy movements, he steadied her upper body, leaned in and ran his tongue in lazy circles around one of her hardened nipples, then the other, before tugging ever so gently with his teeth until she groaned. But there was something else he hungered for even more.

"Stand," he said.

She obeyed.

"Good girl." He slipped her satin pajama bottoms down and let them pool around her feet.

"Did you really say 'good girl'? You have to know that's exactly what I'm determined *not* to be. In fact..."

Before he could do what he really wanted to do, she kneeled between his legs and proceeded to lower his zipper, unleashing his erection from his pants, and kiss the length of him with his underwear still on.

He wanted it so bad, but he craved something else even more.

It took all his strength and willpower to urge her onto the couch, onto her back, where he was determined to pleasure her first.

"No," she said as she pressed against his shoulders.

"Yes," he countered, as he peeled her hands away and gave them a tender squeeze.

They remained locked in a stare. He wasn't going to back down this time.

She gave a single nod, rested her head on the pillow and covered her eyes with both hands. She allowed him the honor, and pleasure, of parting her thighs. Yet another image for his dream file.

With each kiss up the length of her legs, all the way to the sweet juncture, she seemed to simultaneously tense and relax.

He explored her lovely, wet folds until he found that perfect spot. His tongue flicked and circled and consumed her clit with thick-yet-gentle intensity. As soon as he slipped one finger deep inside of her, she released an unmistakable moan and dug her nails into his shoulders.

If only he could make her come a second time this way. He wanted her moans of pleasure to echo off the brick walls of this amazing prison. But as soon as she willingly spread her legs even farther apart and looked down at him with the sweetest pained expression, he knew she needed the same thing he needed.

Now.

The condom he had pocketed for their five o'clock meeting at the club was still tucked inside his pants pocket.

Of course, he hadn't intended to break the cardinal rule. At the same time, he recognized his utter inability to resist her and decided to at least be sensible about the possibility. Thankfully, the day had unfolded the way it had, with her canceling.

Once sheathed, he sat on the couch and shifted her back on his lap. Facing him, even though he'd willingly explore the other alternative.

She took the lead and eased his full length deep inside.

From there, he took over, guiding her hips in slow and measured moves, assuring she got the friction she needed in all the right places while her breasts softly swayed before his hungry eyes.

"Oh, baby," she moaned under her breath.

Her glorious brunette mane fell every which way across her face, chest and shoulders as she threw her head back. Her velvet walls contracted around him as he pressed deeper into her. It took everything he had not to join her.

Instead, he put on the proverbial brakes.

*Look at me.*

She opened her eyes slowly, as if awakening from a peaceful sleep, then leaned in and kissed him. Deeply. She teased his tongue with hers until he nearly exploded. But he didn't want this to be over for either of them. Not yet.

He reluctantly pulled away from the kiss, then resumed moving her hips. He found that perfect pace, that perfect spot, that perfect position that she'd revealed to him and endured his own unbearable pain of needing release until she unleashed the deepest moan. He continued with the same motion and took her there again with even greater intensity, judging by how much hotter and tighter and wetter she suddenly felt.

She stayed on top for the several beyond-glorious seconds of his release that followed. They remained in the same position and held each other in an otherwise loose embrace until their breathing returned to normal.

He eased out of her gently, and she rolled onto the sofa beside him. With what little energy remained, he got up and walked over to a closed door.

"That's the closet. The bathroom's over there," she managed to say.

He found his way and almost threw the condom in the toilet, but course-corrected at the last minute. By the time he came out, she had wrapped herself in the blanket again, her satin pajamas still in an apricot puddle on the floor.

"I was about to ask directions. I promise," he said.

"I'm sure you were."

He pulled his underwear and jeans back on, along with his shirt. The whole sequence screamed "booty call complete" since she hadn't invited him to spend the night.

He'd taken a huge chance by showing up unannounced. The next move was hers.

He sat beside her, and she leaned into him again.

"I'm starving," she said.

The blanket slipped, exposing one of her bare shoulders.

He could definitely go another round tonight. After

an extended recharge time, of course. But he was pretty sure the bare shoulder was an accident, rather than an invitation.

"I interrupted your delicious soup, didn't I?" he said.

"You interrupted more than the broth, which was cooked to perfection, by the way. You also interrupted my dessert."

"Dessert?"

With her index finger, she traced a line from his chest to his navel, and then down the length of his zipper.

*Oh, that.*

"I'm the guest, you're the hostess. Next time you're at my house, I'll serve whatever dessert you want. I promise."

"Okay, then. I'm coming over tonight," she said, but her yawn indicated otherwise.

"Let's make it tomorrow night. You're exhausted. And I'm depleted, if you catch my drift." He was about to pull the blanket back over her, but Baby jumped on the couch and claimed it. Which gave him an idea.

"How 'bout I take Baby home with me so you can get some rest?"

She took her time considering the offer. In fact, she took a little too much time.

"Not tonight. Besides, I wouldn't want you to get too attached, since we're trying to find her a forever home."

Too late. He was already attached. To both of them, apparently. Which meant he better leave before he fell any deeper. Leave it at booty call, until otherwise notified.

"Dinner tomorrow? I'll take you out. Show you off," he said.

*Stupid is back in the race, and is now ahead by three furlongs.*

"Sure. Unless the migraine makes an encore. I'll call or text."

"Perfect." He planted a kiss on her forehead and stood to leave.

Not exactly perfect. He was going for an enthusiastic "yes."

At least her handy excuse made it easier to walk out the door tonight. He already had one foot out of this city, in theory, which felt like a much bigger step than it had before. But any kind of "yes" from area code 850 would put both feet on solid ground.

Equestrian training ground, to be specific.

If he wanted to lead a respectable life ever again, it was his only option.

# *11*

THE BLANKET KIRBY had stayed wrapped in all night might as well have been a tangled web of unanswered questions.

The migraine had mercifully dissolved, and any lingering doubt about her desirability had been put to rest by this gorgeous man.

What hadn't gone away was a certainty that he was hiding something about the club. He had blatantly dodged her comment about the other guys sleeping with their clients. If nothing was going on, why wouldn't he simply deny it? And if the club was really on the up and up, how did he get access to her address?

*Talking in my sleep?* Doubtful.

Maybe tonight she could pursue more answers, even though at this juncture she wasn't sure what she'd do with the information. Her emotions were hopelessly entangled, and her head was a total mess. No migraine required.

At least she'd unearthed one truth when she got the confession from Madison. Hopefully, she'd snag a second with the saddles. Eventually, she'd tell Adam what she'd discovered. He deserved to know the truth. But telling him how she'd known about Madison in the first place? *That* would require a level of disclosure she couldn't give until her investigation of the club was complete.

She'd sent an email to Todd Kelly right after Adam had left last night, inquiring about any Hermès saddles he might own. Todd's response was waiting in her inbox by the time she woke up. Madison had given him one for his birthday last year, and bought one for herself. She allegedly used some of her trust-fund money for the purchases. Todd had asked her to return them. Too extravagant, he said. Besides, they specialized in Western, not English saddle. Of course, that hurt her feelings, and the last thing he wanted to do was upset her further. Todd decided to let it rest for the time being. Now, it seemed, Kirby was stirring up the dust again. Fortunately, Todd was being an excellent sport about it.

She fixed a cup of coffee, shot a reply to Todd requesting he check the serial numbers, then sat back and sipped the brew from the same mug in which Adam had served her the chicken broth.

His vanilla-and-pine scent lingered on her skin, and her entire body still ached at the thought of the way his hands had guided her hips with such confidence and precision. How he'd introduced her to multiple orgasms for the first time in her life.

Her thoughts zeroed in on the places he had touched and kissed. Especially the way his tongue and fingers had probed and explored her depths with tender enthusiasm.

She reached for her cell phone and texted, Are we on for tonight?

His response was immediate.

Definitely. Pick you up at 7.

What should I wear?

Your prettiest, most easily removable dress.

The subsequent thrill from his response stayed with her as she showered, dressed and drove to the station. The high lasted up until the moment she reached her desk, only to find Seth sitting in her chair.

"What are you doing?" she asked.

"I'm snooping."

Panic settled in her throat, heavy and spiked with dread. Had she failed to log off again? What, exactly, had she put in her notes about Adam?

She practically ran around behind him, only to find nothing but a blank screen.

"Ha! Gotcha," he said.

Her heavy exhale spoke volumes. She couldn't have disguised her relief if she'd wanted.

"You do have something on The Deep. Care to fill me in on the child-molester-turned-prostitute?"

She shoved her purse into a drawer.

"I'm investigating the club, not the man," she said, even though that wasn't true. She was juggling both. "There's nothing solid to report at this time, aside from some good-looking guys playing therapist to broken-hearted women. I promise to keep you posted."

"Adam Drake is a known offender. And, news flash, there's even more to his story. In fact, I'm thinking of launching a separate investigation."

She braced herself for yet another revelation.

"What do you mean, 'more to his story'?"

"Apparently, some expensive saddles have gone missing, and Drake is the prime suspect."

*Yes, I know.*

"Where did you hear that?"

Seth smiled and backed away. "Oh, no. I'm not giving away any more secrets. Not when you've been, shall we say, less than forthcoming."

"I am already aware of the saddle situation, and the allegations by the Beckers. I'm also aware of your other secret."

Well, at least one of his secrets. The guy probably had a closet full of them, but the only one that interested her was how Todd Kelly had tried to get Seth to issue a retraction, and Seth had ignored the guy.

No matter what Seth had seen on her computer—and judging from the blank screen, he hadn't seen anything—she could call him out on his lie, if necessary. She was tempted to confront him now, but she couldn't afford to be impulsive. She still had several truths she was chasing down about the club, about the saddles. About what exactly was happening between Adam and her, and was it real or fleeting. She didn't need Seth pressuring her or complicating matters. What she did need was more time.

And only one man could make that happen.

Kirby knocked on the door frame of Bettencourt's office.

Even though his open-door policy was widely known, she never felt comfortable barging in and taking a seat, as she'd seen Seth do a million times. Maybe it was because the news director always had a frantic, don't-bother-me look about him, from the top of his too-thick, too-white hair to the bottom of his running-shoe soles.

When he didn't look away from his computer screen or say a word, she asked, "May I talk with you for a minute?"

Bettencourt swiveled to face her and peered over the top edge of his reading glasses. "Ah! My favorite prodigy. Of course."

She closed the door behind her and eased into one of the two chairs opposite his desk.

"I wanted to update you on The Deep," she said.

"What do you have so far?"

"Mostly suspicion."

"For good reason, based on what information your lead offered."

"I'm still working on it, but I don't have enough facts to prove it's even a story worth telling."

As soon as she phrased it that way, she regretted mentioning it. That wasn't even the point she'd intended to make, coming in. Was her conscience looking for an emergency exit?

"Well, it has only been a few days, hasn't it? But I have to be straight with you, Kirby. Seth has been champing at the bit to take on this piece. This is the type of story he lives for. If you don't feel you're up to this, I'll let him take a stab at it."

The suggestion set off major alarms. Handing the assignment over to Seth would be the worst thing she could do to Adam. And to her career. The Deep was her lead. Her story. Period.

"I can handle it. Problem is, Seth seems to think there's major dirt on my contact. If he goes after that angle, it could compromise my ongoing investigation. That's my biggest concern, and why I wanted to talk to you."

"Is that what he's up to? He didn't come right out and

say it, but I knew there was something churning around in that head of his. He's not exactly opaque."

"That's putting it mildly."

Bettencourt offered up a half smile, then removed his reading glasses and leaned forward on his elbows.

"Look, Kirby, Seth can't help himself. He chases blood, literally and figuratively. He's got an extraordinary nose for this business. But what makes him great at his job is the same thing that trips him up. He's too impulsive, whereas you're the furthest thing from it. I need to merge the two of you, and then I'd have the perfect reporter."

The thought of merging with Seth, even figuratively, was enough to make her dry-heave. But what Bettencourt was implying was even more disturbing.

Had she really become too cautious? Was coming in here to voice her concerns a mistake? A sign of weakness, when she'd tried so hard to be strong and objective? Besides, she'd been impulsive once. It didn't turn out well for her. She had the emotional scars to prove it.

Kirby sat up straighter.

"I refuse to air false information or pure conjecture. I'm simply asking for enough time to secure any evidence. If it turns out that there isn't any evidence to secure, I'll properly wrap up the assignment and put it to bed. For now, I want your assurance that Seth won't be allowed to investigate my contact."

Bettencourt put his cheaters back on and peered over the top of the frames.

"Okay. I won't hold you to a hard deadline, but keep digging. Dig until you strike gold because it's there. I can smell it. This whole club concept has 'debauchery' written all over it. Get this one right, and your star will outshine Seth's. But that's just between you and me."

With that, he swiveled back around and returned to his task, as if what he'd said wasn't a big deal.

It was a *huge* deal for Kirby. The vote of confidence alone made her feel as though she'd already struck gold.

The extra time would allow her to get as much information as she needed on The Deep. It would also give her time to find out more about the missing saddles, even though she was almost 100 percent sure Todd Kelly would come through with a match.

Get this one right? No worries there. She had every intention of getting it right.

All of it.

"Love is making you soft, man," Fabian said as he slapped Adam on the back.

His sweaty back.

"On the contrary, Fab. I've been quite hard lately." He added a smile for the full effect.

Fabian acknowledged the innuendo with a smirk and a nod.

Adam walked to the free weights and grabbed a pair of forty-five pounders.

Fabian grabbed the same weight, but he couldn't even accomplish one curl.

"Don't laugh," Fabian said as he replaced the weights in the stand and seemed to contemplate his limit.

"Grab the pink ones, cupcake," Adam said, referring to the five pounders. "Let me know if you need me to spot you."

"Very funny, Ride. I don't have the same motivation as you. Besides, I don't have to look as good for the ladies. The leftovers aren't that picky."

"Damn, Fab, could your standards be any lower?"

The statement brought back thoughts of last night,

when one of Adam's clients ran her fake nails over his biceps and down his arm while commenting on how strong he was. Instead of feeling good, if had felt creepy.

He replaced the forty-fivers with some fifties.

Fabian shook his head. "So, what's she like?"

"Who?" Adam asked, his mind still in the nightmare client's clawlike grip.

"Kirby."

Adam didn't want to go there. He'd tried hard to separate this relationship thing with Kirby from the club part of his life. If only he'd met her a couple of years ago, when he had an honorable career.

"I don't really know much about her."

*Except that she's smart, funny, has the most beautiful face and the tightest, most responsive body.*

An inconvenient hard-on threatened to reveal the trajectory of his thoughts before he could fully enjoy it.

"How booked am I for tomorrow night?" Adam asked. If anything could reverse a hard-on, it was a heavy workload at The Deep.

"Booked solid. Didn't help that you're flaking out tonight. I had to reschedule a few, with no room to spare. Many tears were shed, my friend."

"Maybe you could take my place, since they aren't that picky."

"Very true. Or Gentleman John can fill in for both of us. Literally."

Adam snorted.

"I'm glad rebooking the ladies didn't cause you too much grief, Fab. Wouldn't want you to have to actually work or anything."

At least Adam had tonight to look forward to. Hopefully, by the end of the evening, he'd know a lot more about Kirby, which was an extralarge reason to take her out rather than have dinner at his place again.

Whether finding out what was beneath that beautiful surface of hers ended up being good or bad, at least he'd have a better direction because he intended to play his best hand, lay a few more cards on the table and place his bets with this one.

"I gotta be honest, Ride. There's something about her I don't trust," Fabian said.

The guy sure knew how to spoil a mood. What he lacked in discretion, he made up for in superb timing.

"Why?"

Fabian replaced the weights on the rack and rested his hands on his hips. "I don't know. I can't put my finger on it. She's different than the others who come in."

"I know. That's why I like her. And she confided in me about why she booked time. She's legit. Don't worry, she's not the reporter."

As he said it, a microsecond of doubt pricked his conscience. He almost wished she hadn't revealed her dream career to him. Now, it colored his view of everything.

"Did she now? When did she have time to do all this confiding? Oh, that's right, you stalked her last night."

"I stopped by her loft to check on her."

"And she confessed her life story?"

"No, she confided in me earlier."

"Did she pay you? Because Lydia will be pissed if she finds out you're taking business away from the club."

"She won't be coming back to the club. And she didn't pay me, Fab. Everything has been reciprocal."

Well, almost everything. She practically begged for the dessert he had to offer, and far be it from him to deny her for much longer.

"What, exactly, does she do for a living?" Fabian asked.

"Some sort of desk job. But she dreams of something better."

"Don't we all."

"Amen," Adam said.

"So, where exactly is this desk located? FBI or CIA headquarters, by chance? Or maybe she's with CNN or the *National Enquirer*."

"You're being paranoid, Fab."

"And you're being reckless, Ride. Fuck her all you want, but don't go confiding in her. Not this soon. Not with the possibility of a traitor in our midst. I recommend you find out more about her. A lot more."

Discussion over. What went on behind the red door at the club was the least of Adam's worries. Except, yes, Kirby seemed a little curious. More than a little. He'd chalked it up as interest in him, but maybe he wasn't taking it seriously enough.

In any case, she might eventually find out a lot more about him. He hadn't confided in her about his newest high-ticket problem. Sure, she believed and supported his version regarding the harassment allegations. But if he kept piling on his problems, she'd eventually get worn down from the sheer volume.

To everyone else, it probably wouldn't matter that he didn't steal the saddles. Just like it didn't matter that he didn't sexually harass a client. To everyone else, he was guilty.

Even when he wasn't.

# 12

"MAKE YOURSELF AT home while I finish getting ready." Kirby sweetened the request with her knockout smile.

Adam never did mind waiting for a woman to finish getting dressed. It was the getting undressed part where he seriously lacked patience. Besides, Kirby's loft already felt like home, especially with the way Baby greeted him at the door.

He could get used to this. All of it.

For now, he wanted nothing more than to rip that black minidress completely off her body. Hopefully, the getting-dressed part was complete, even though her outfit appeared mercilessly incomplete.

Damn, did she have some amazing thighs. Strong, tan and oh, so spreadable. He watched those legs, and the rest of her gorgeous body, disappear into the adjacent room.

He shed his jacket and laid it across the back of the oversized taupe velvet couch.

Velvet. Like every last inch of her.

The thoughts he'd managed to suppress clawed to the forefront of his brain. His cock responded to the image of him removing her clothes and diving into her wet velvet warmth.

Short of hijacking her bathroom and taking an ice-cold shower, the best way to turn off his hard-on might be to look around while he waited.

He walked over to a bookcase positioned against the exposed brick wall and studied the titles. True crime books by Ann Rule ruled, with biographies of politicians and rock stars coming in second.

Occasionally, a framed photo interrupted the rank-and-file flow of the myriad nonfiction hardbacks. The symmetry of the bookcase was either well-planned or brilliantly intuitive. Everything seemed balanced, every space utilized.

One photo in particular caught his eye. A photo of a young family. The mother and father sat next to each other on a love seat. The man's face was turned toward the woman, who balanced a little girl on her knee as they both stared directly into the camera. Besides wearing matching pale pink shift dresses, they also wore matching smiles.

Yep, that had to be Kirby.

His chest constricted and he could barely breathe. He'd had a similar photo taken with his parents. A moment frozen in time, before time ripped the family apart and took his parents away forever. The remaining photos of his childhood would be of him and his grandfather, Henry, a widower who had to play all the familial roles for the only survivor of that two-car crash.

"That's me, my mom and my dad," she said as she came up behind him.

"Do they live in Houston?"

"My father lives in Bay City. My mom passed away the week after that photo was taken. Aneurism."

Adam placed the photo back on the shelf and took her in his arms. Considering his own tragic past, he should have known better than to make any assumptions.

"I'm sorry," he said. He backed it up with a respectable kiss on those glossy pink lips.

*Strawberry.*

Either he was getting a major buzz from the taste of her, or his phone was vibrating in his pocket.

"Mmm. That's an interesting response," she said as she pressed into him.

"Excuse me for a sec." He retrieved the phone and glanced at the number. *Wild Indigo.* Maybe they'd made their choice. Then again, what if they had more questions? What if their decision hinged upon it?

He couldn't talk to them now. And certainly not here. Other questions needed to be answered first.

He slipped the phone back into his pocket and let the message roll to voice mail.

"Not important?" she asked.

He ran his hand up and down her back.

"It's nothing that can't wait. Let's get out of here before I undo all of your hard work to look so stunning," he said. Not to mention before he got distracted from following the only good advice Fabian had ever offered.

Find out everything he could about Kirby Montgomery.

KIRBY STARED ACROSS the cozy table for two at the most handsome man she'd ever seen. He looked good in nothing but his bare skin, but he looked even better in a suit jacket.

Well, maybe not better. Different.

She'd never really studied his face from this angle— straight on—except during those brief moments that ended in a make-out session, or during the longer moments of lovemaking. In a way, she felt less exposed when naked, with him pressed against her and into her. Under the lights of downtown Houston's trendiest steak house, there were fewer places to hide.

Adam seemed completely comfortable, judging by the way he leaned back slightly and looked at her from across the table.

Neither of them spoke as a waiter uncorked a bottle of Silver Oak cabernet and allowed Adam to approve the wine. After the waiter poured both glasses, he quieted away to another table.

Adam raised his glass. "To our second official date."

She echoed his toast, although it felt as though they'd been dating for weeks. The club, the grocery store, his house. Her loft.

"The booty call doesn't count as a date?" she teased.

"It definitely counts for something."

She took a sip of wine, willing the warmth to soothe her nerves. It didn't help that she'd forgotten to put away her company Christmas party photo, sitting on her bookshelf. She wasn't quite ready to explain it.

Fortunately, she hadn't had to, but it had been a close call.

"Hey, you. Did I say something wrong?" Adam's deep voice pulled her out of her thoughts.

"Not at all. I was just overthinking. I do that quite often."

"I noticed. And I'm perfectly fine with it, as long as I get a portion of your thoughts."

His eyes seemed to take inventory of her responses. It was something she wasn't used to. Her ex always took in everything else, and everyone else, when they went out. She could have disappeared for thirty minutes and he wouldn't have known she was gone. For some reason, she got used to it. Even accepted it.

But Adam? Adam was attentive. And beautiful.

"Tell me more about the real Kirby Montgomery. You mentioned a desk job. What industry?" He took a sip of wine.

The question didn't seem like an idle one. It wasn't the worst thing he could have asked, but it came in a close second. He could have asked for the name of her employer.

"Oil and gas, at the moment."

Not the whole truth, but not a complete lie, either. Aside from her attempt at investigative reporting on The Deep, she focused on cultivating other leads, including oil and gas, then distributing them to Seth and the other field reporters.

Adam seemed content with the answer, but the way he pinched his brows together suggested the interrogation was only beginning.

"When you say 'at the moment,' what do you mean?"

The warm tingling in her belly from minutes ago now felt blistering under his intense gaze. *Maybe that's why he tends to burn dinner.*

"I see my desk job as a temporary situation. Like I mentioned, my dream is to become a reporter."

"Yes, I remember you saying that," he said.

"And I remember you weren't too fond of the idea," she countered.

He nodded.

Thankfully, the waiter placed a basket of fresh bread between them, along with a trio of condiments—butter, olive oil and something she couldn't identify. The interruption provided a segue to a safer topic. A parachute down from the edge and onto terra firma.

"May I ask you something?" she said.

"I suppose it's your turn to interrogate." He tore off a piece of bread, dipped it in the olive oil and offered it to her, then peeled off a larger chunk for himself.

She held the bread in one hand instead of eating it.

"Why did you choose the name 'Easy Ride'? You must realize how it sounds."

He nearly choked on his bite of bread.

"'Cowboy Roy' was already taken."

"Seriously?"

He shook his head. "'Easy Ride' is a reference to horses. The love of my life is a schooling horse named Daisy. I've always referred to her as an 'easy ride' because she's so gentle and caring with the students."

Adam's wistful smile wasn't lost on her. Clearly, this particular creature meant the world to him.

"So, your moniker was straightforward from the beginning," she said.

"Yes, but that doesn't make me innocent. I fully intended to take advantage of the innuendo and my position at the club. I was fresh out of a bad relationship, and my career was on the rocks."

"What stopped you?" she asked.

"I immediately knew I wasn't cut out for it. I'd hear these relationship horror stories from the women, and some of them sounded remarkably similar to mine."

She tilted her head, swirled the wine in her glass and asked the question she had to ask.

"But the other guys take advantage all the time, don't they?"

He leaned back and seemed to measure her question.

"I don't know about that," he finally said. "I tend to think it's the clients who take advantage. They come to us. Not the other way around. They get whatever it is they need, and then they're gone."

The implication hit hard and fast. He might as well have stripped her bare and turned up the lights. That had been her intention. To get in and out of the club with the story. To take what she needed, and then leave.

Except, she was still there. Furthermore, she didn't want to go anywhere.

"I've taken advantage of you," she said.

He cocked his head. "How so?"

"You paid for my groceries, you cooked the most thoughtful dinner for me at your house, you didn't take my money at the club, the one and only time I was there."

*I've used you to get information for a story...*

He leaned forward, taking her hand in his.

"Kirby, I wanted to do all those things for you. And I didn't take your money that night because I broke my own personal rule."

"The one about not making the first move?"

"No. The other one."

"Other?"

He squeezed her hand and looked at her with the softest baby blues. "The one about not falling for a client."

She swallowed hard.

Falling. That breathless, terrifying, exhilarating feeling of heading uncontrollably to a place unknown. Ready or not.

She was falling for him, too. She simply hadn't been brave or truthful, or perhaps impulsive enough to label it.

The waiter returned and proceeded to tick through a list of specials as if he hadn't walked into the middle of an intimate moment. Adam softly smiled at her. Was he even listening to the man?

When the waiter asked if they were ready to order, Adam said, "I think we know what we want."

Even though his words could describe many of her feelings at that moment, Kirby was pretty sure she knew what he meant.

She smiled and nodded.

"We'll have the porterhouse steak for two. Medium," Adam said.

"Except, burn the edges, please," she added.

"Yes, ma'am. Any sides?"

"Asparagus," they said in unison.

As soon as the waiter relieved them of their menus, Adam stood and extended his hand.

"What?" she asked.

"We're going to dance. What else?"

"There isn't a dance floor."

"Then we'll make one," he said.

Kirby looked around. They would pretty much have to dance in place, next to their table. Not that she would mind being seen dancing with him. But she didn't want to embarrass him.

"I don't dance. At least, not very well. I'm pretty sure you witnessed that."

"We have to dance," he said. "They're playing our song."

*"Baby Blue."*

TALK ABOUT EXQUISITE TORTURE. From the slow dance on, Adam battled with his libido to not reveal how turned-on he felt.

He ravaged the dinner under the excuse of having missed lunch, while she wanted to savor every burned edge and talk about their first date at his house.

Hell, he hadn't stopped thinking through those details. But all he could think about over dinner was how much he wanted to unzip her dress. Or, better yet, lift her short hem high enough to sink himself into her warm, velvety depths.

He didn't even attempt to disguise his urgency as he hurried her down the long cement hallway to her loft. Their footsteps must have sounded like the Running of the Bulls.

Now inside, his full hard-on refused to be tamed by logical thoughts.

Baby put his libido temporarily in check as soon as the little mop-headed puppy tried to jump into his arms.

"Not to brag, but Baby seems to prefer me," he said.

"I don't hold that against her. But I'm the alpha in this house. She can have what's left of you after I'm finished."

Kirby shut the door behind them, sidestepped her four-legged competition and swiftly claimed victory by fully embracing him.

She initiated the kiss this time, devouring his lower lip first before dipping her tongue slowly into his mouth.

He reciprocated, and their tongues did the slow, lazy, perfect dance that came so naturally. Maybe Kirby wasn't much on the dance floor, but her exquisite mouth and intuitive tongue more than made up for it.

She pulled away, took his hand and led him to the next room. Her bedroom.

He hadn't seen this space last time. They hadn't made it any farther than the taupe velvet sofa. This room was dark, except for a high horizontal window that allowed some moonlight in from outside. Not nearly enough for his taste, however. The light from the main room helped illuminate half the bed, which he mentally assigned to her.

"Stay," she commanded. She sat at the end of the bed while he remained standing.

"Come," she said as she reached for his belt loops and tugged him into position between her legs.

He obeyed.

"Good boy," she said with a sexy, bad-girl grin.

Alpha suited her nicely, he decided.

She unbuckled his belt, slipped it out of the loops and dropped it to the floor.

He attempted to unzip his pants because she was taking way too long, but she pushed aside his hands.

She looked up from her task. "No."

"I'm the guest. It should be my choice," he said, suspecting where this seduction was leading.

She unhooked, unzipped and peeled down his slacks until they rested around his feet.

"I'm the hostess. You'll graciously accept what I have to offer."

She tugged his underwear down to the floor and ran her hands along the side of his bare hips, taking him in visually.

As soon as she touched him, as soon as her delicate hand traveled the length of his shaft, he threw his head back and closed his eyes. And prayed that he'd last more than ten seconds because he could feel a welling of pressure deep within.

Her breath warmed him, and he groaned when she ran her tongue up his length. Her tongue circled the head, touching upon the vulnerable underside. As she began to take him into her velvet mouth, he pulled away.

It wasn't that he didn't want to go further. Having her want this so badly validated him to the core. Rather, he wanted the most intimate connection with her at the moment.

He eased her shoulders back, her feet still solid on the ground and her legs open to him.

"Stay," he said as he reached to the floor to retrieve a condom from his pants pocket.

"I wasn't finished," she said as she attempted to prop herself back up on her elbows.

He urged her back down. "I wouldn't have lasted."

He fell to his knees and rolled on the latex, which bought him some time. But now? Now, he wanted what he saw spread out before him.

*This.* The ease in which he penetrated her with his full length, and with one single focused thrust, was enough to convince him that he hadn't been totally selfish by bulldozing past foreplay. She was turned on, as well.

He willed himself to last a little longer and reached between them and gently massaged her clit, circling her with his thumb while continuing to ease fully in and out at a slow, steady pace.

"Look at me," he said.

She did. Her longing gaze, her labored breathing and the arousing rise and fall of her chest made it hard for him to not explode.

"How does that feel?" he managed to ask. It sure felt damn good to him.

She didn't answer. She didn't have to. Once again, her body answered for her. She arched her back and opened herself to him, even farther. Her expression looked so beautifully pained.

He wanted nothing more than to move faster and faster. Deeper and deeper. Instead, he maintained the long, slow, easy pace that seemed to take her there, and savored the benefit of her unmistakable release.

He leaned in and pressed fully into her—chest to

chest, lips to lips, heat to heat—and kissed her deeply as he joined her with one final, gloriously selfish thrust.

After he caught his breath, he pulled away. One day, he'd stay connected with her all night.

She scooted back, still wearing that beautiful cocktail dress.

"Let me help you get out of that before it gets too wrinkled." He joined her on the bed, reached around and tugged on the zipper.

"How thoughtful of you."

"I'm unselfish that way."

He lay back as she stood to shed the dress. The slight flare of the bottom half parachuted to the floor, revealing those full natural breasts. No bra.

Seeing her standing before him—so simple and immediate and without reservation—nearly floored him. Although her shyness turned him on, this more confident version could bring a dead man back to life.

Like the intoxicating contradiction she was, she eased under the covers, then pulled them over her breasts.

He got up, disposed of the condom and walked to the main room, where he checked his phone message from Wild Indigo. No questions after all. Only a promise that they'd give him an answer soon.

He switched off the lights and settled back in beside her. Completely exhausted and totally satisfied.

He did have one more question, which had been traipsing through his head practically since day one. Now was as good a time as any to ask.

"I was thinking," he began. "I'd like to adopt Baby if you haven't already lined up a home."

Kirby kissed him on the cheek.

*Was that a yes?*

"You don't have to answer tonight. Give it some

thought," he said, although he'd sleep a lot better if he knew Baby was officially his. Even though he'd given it plenty of consideration, it still felt impulsive as hell. End of the day, he'd provide a good home, if not a structured one.

"Yes," she whispered. "Is there any other answer?"

Damn if this wasn't the best ending to the best night he'd had in long time. He, for one, could barely stay awake.

However, in the semi-darkness of the room, he could tell her eyes remained open. Obviously, she was overthinking again.

Question was, were the thoughts good?

As soon as Kirby felt sure Adam was asleep, she slid out from beneath the covers, grabbed his button-down shirt from the edge of the bed, slipped it on and tiptoed out of the bedroom.

Nothing would be better than staying right there, in his arms, for the entire night. But she needed to do something before he woke up.

She closed the door only partially to avoid engaging the squeaky hinges, and headed straight for the bookcase. There, on the top shelf, sat the group photo that had been taken at the Christmas party last year, with her standing next to Seth.

If only she could reach high enough to grab it. She was able to slide the corner of the frame toward her. It wobbled on its back leg, but it didn't fall down.

She needed a ladder, but she didn't have one of those. Instead, she picked up an ottoman and placed it in front of the shelves. She somehow balanced on the soft platform long enough to secure the photo.

She'd barely stepped down when Baby jetted from the bedroom, barking the entire way.

"Shh!"

The reprimand only made Baby bark louder.

Kirby padded to the kitchen area. As she tried to find a suitable hiding place for the photo, the overhead lights flashed on.

Adam stood there, completely naked. His beauty and raw power made her almost forget why she had gotten up in the first place. But the cold, sharp edges of the frame bit into her bare chest, reminding her. She pressed it firmly against her, unable to cover the evidence with his shirt.

"Is everything okay?" he asked.

"I couldn't sleep, and I didn't want to disturb you. I came out here and was going to get on my computer, but Baby came in and started barking."

Adam ran a hand through his hair as he took a few steps toward her.

"Your computer is over there. What are you holding?"

She gripped the frame even tighter.

He looked at the misplaced ottoman, then up to the shelf, then back at her. "Is there something you don't want me to see?"

She shook her head, for lack of something to say. She could tell by his expression that silence wasn't the right answer. Unfortunately, there wasn't a right answer.

"You and Baby go back to bed. I'll be there in a minute."

"What time is it?" he asked.

She glanced at the clock on the microwave. "One thirty."

He nodded. "Maybe I should go back to my place. Let you get some sleep. Obviously, I'm intruding."

"You're not intruding."

"Then what are you hiding? If it's a picture of you and your ex, or whoever it might be, I can handle it."

"It's not an ex."

"Then what is it? I thought we agreed to be open."

He stepped closer, pried the photo from her grip and took a good hard look at it.

"So you know this scumbag?"

This time, she didn't nod or shake her head. She felt paralyzed.

"Oh. Wait. I get it. You work with him. Or maybe for him," Adam said.

"I… Yes. I work with him."

"At a desk."

"The assignments desk."

"Great," he said as he slapped the photo down on the counter. "I need to get out of here for a while."

"I thought you said you could handle it. Whatever it is."

He shook his head, turned around and walked into the bedroom.

Baby ran after him, with Kirby a close second.

"I'm sorry. I didn't want to scare you off after you mentioned his name," she said.

He paused from picking up his clothes.

"I wouldn't have held it against you, Kirby. But you outright lied to me. Which makes me wonder what else you're lying about."

"I didn't lie."

He searched the floor for his pants, then shook them out and put them on as if he couldn't get dressed fast enough.

"That's a stretch, and you know it. Oil and gas? Really? But never mind, let's call it withholding instead. You're familiar with the concept, aren't you?"

Was he really going there, of all places? The possibility provoked her defenses.

"You weren't exactly open with me. You withheld information, too. Anything else you'd like to tell me about Madison Kel—" Kirby inhaled sharply as soon as she realized her mistake.

Those blue eyes of his narrowed in on her.

"How the hell do you know her name? And when did this become about me?"

She wanted to explain exactly how she knew, and that she had every intention of telling him everything at some point. But, at the moment, she didn't know what to say.

In the long stretch of her silence, his expression changed from one of confusion to one of enlightenment.

"All this is about me, isn't it? It's been about me the whole time. You're the reporter we were all warned about. I can't believe I've been so fucking blind. You and Wainwright weren't satisfied with ruining my career at Becker Farms. Now you want to see how much more you can take from me by going after The Deep."

"No, that's not it."

"Are you the reporter or aren't you?"

"I was assigned to investigate The Deep, but I'm not trying to take anything from you. I swear, Adam."

He took a few angry steps toward her.

"What the *hell* do you think will happen to me if there's any negative publicity?"

She couldn't answer, even though she knew in her heart what could happen.

"Let me fill you in. It will ruin the only chance I have for a better life." Adam shook his head. "Something about you didn't feel right from that very first night. Or I guess it felt too right, which should have been a clue."

He located his jacket and slipped it on.

She grabbed his sleeve. "Please don't leave. Let me explain."

"Stop it, Kirby. I'm not as stupid as you seem to think," he said as he tore away from her grip and retrieved his belt and shoes.

"I never thought you were stupid. But you hid something, too. Neither of us is innocent here."

He smiled one of those I-can't-fucking-believe-I'm-hearing-this smiles.

"I told you I had legal problems. But that explains why the drawer was cracked open, and how you must have gotten Madison's name. Did you get up in the middle of the night to snoop, or did you wait until I took Baby for a walk?"

"I accidentally came across the papers when you took Baby for a walk. Are you happy? Then I pulled the papers out and looked at them, like how you pulled the photo from my grip and looked at it."

"Don't you dare compare that to what you did."

He towered over her.

"Tell me, Kirby. If that's even your real name. Was the abusive-ex-husband bullshit part of your act? Because that's the way this particular story is piecing together for me."

"Please, Adam," she said, though she found it hard to even breathe. "Give me a chance."

"You had your chance, and I'm not a big believer in seconds. Do me a favor. Don't explain anything. Ever again. Oh, and you can keep the shirt. I don't want it anymore."

*Oh, God. This is it. This is what the end of a perfect*

*relationship feels like. A giant, angry fist, straight to the heart.*

She felt too weak to argue. Too shredded to come up with anything that could save her. Save them. So she watched him leave. Watched as he took a moment to gently pat Baby on the head, and felt grateful for that one thing. His anger toward her didn't spill over to the innocent puppy.

Then she and Baby watched as he slammed the door behind him.

Kirby collapsed into a damp heap on the floor and sobbed herself to sleep.

The next morning, she stood on uncertain legs, took a deep breath and made a decision. As soon as she got to work, she wouldn't just bury her notes on The Deep. She would delete them forever.

## 13

"WHAT HAPPENED TO YOU?" Seth asked.

For once, Kirby wasn't the least bit bothered by his less-than-flattering observations. She knew she looked horrible. It was to be expected of a person who'd single-handedly ruined her own life.

"I'm on my period. Any other questions?"

Her thoughts traveled back to that morning in the grocery store. She'd looked hideous, yet Adam easily and willingly handled the pink box, and more than willingly handled her.

She put a quick, tight leash on the tears and switched on her computer. There, front and center, sat her folder of notes on the story. It had been her ticket to greater things at one time.

Now, it offered nothing but a reminder of every wrong turn she'd taken.

She dragged the folder and its contents to the trash and emptied the digital wastebasket, feeling as empty and worthless as the icon itself.

Her cell phone dinged, alerting her to a new text message.

*Reese.* Not the message she wanted, and she couldn't summon the energy to text Reese in return.

Not that she expected Adam to respond to her apology or plea or explanation. He'd made himself very clear.

What would she explain anyway? No matter how she arranged the words in her head, they all spelled *deceit.* Even her dyslexia couldn't transpose them into making some kind of sense.

Seth sauntered back after refilling his superlarge ceramic mug with coffee.

"I'm worried about you, Kirby. Can I do anything to help? Need me to take this assignment off your plate? I can go at it from another angle. No need for you to get any further involved."

Whereas she was good at facial expressions, Seth was a certified expert at reading other people's pain.

"Not necessary. I'm on it."

Even though she'd effectively thrown away her one chance at this story, she intended to make use of that rope Bettencourt had extended, and hang on for dear life until she could figure out something.

She started by booking an appointment with Adam at The Deep. Finally, a lucky break. One available time slot. *And it's mine.* With a tap of a key, she was in. Besides, she needed a shoulder to cry on, more than ever. And he would be getting paid. He'd have no choice but to listen.

She had to tell him that Madison Kelly had recanted her accusation, and Todd Kelly confirmed in an email this morning that the serial numbers matched up. Of course, that would only prove she'd been snooping even deeper into his business.

She'd definitely tell Bettencourt everything she'd discovered, in case Seth got any bright ideas to pursue that angle after all.

"Why don't you take the rest of the day off, Montgomery? Bettencourt isn't even here this morning. As soon as he gets back, I'll let him know you aren't feeling well and that I'm covering for you."

For once, she agreed with him.

She collected her purse and hauled her sleep-deprived, undernourished, sorry ass out the door and directly home, where she would think of a way to make everything up to Adam.

Or, yet again, cry herself to sleep trying.

ADAM READ EVERY word of the document from his attorney regarding the newest allegations about the saddles.

Liars. The world was filled with them. Still, if he couldn't beat them, he refused to join them.

His cell phone vibrated. Fabian to the rescue.

"You better be calling with some good news," Adam said.

"I don't know whether it's good, but it's news you'll be glad to hear. I've rebooked all your customers from last night. You're looking at a full plate the next few days."

"Whatever."

"What is up with you?"

"Trying to get some personal paperwork done," Adam said as he massaged his temple.

"Or, maybe your girlfriend is there today?"

"She's not my girlfriend."

"She's obviously something. Or wants to be. She booked time with you tonight. Private room. Prime time, eight o'clock. Or, as I always say, sloppy-seconds o'clock. Thought the news might cheer you up."

Cheer him up? The whole idea of it slammed him down.

"Cancel her."

"Is the honeymoon over already? Then why would she book you?"

"Who cares? I don't want to see her. I have the right to decline an appointment."

"Yes, you do. Okay, Ride. I'll put her with someone else. It's kinda sounding as if she might require a new shoulder to cry on anyway."

Even though he knew he shouldn't care, the thought of her with someone else cut to the core.

"Fab. Delete her account. Don't give her access to anyone. She's the reporter."

"Wait… What? Did you say 'reporter'? What the—"

"Sorry, man. I just found out myself."

"Holy crap. So it wasn't a rumor. How much did you tell her?"

"I don't remember."

The sound of Fabian's panicked fingers banging against the touch screen almost drowned out his symphony of curse words. Almost.

"I'm deleting her as we speak, and with great pleasure. She'll get a notice that her appointment has been canceled, and she'll be locked out of her account. I'll reset the door code, as well, so 181 is S-O-L."

"Again, sorry. I thought she was a nice girl."

"Ride, you really are a hopeless romantic. Nice girls don't sleep with guys like us. And the really nice ones don't end up screwing us over."

"Yeah, yeah. I hear you. Don't tell Lydia. Yet."

"Oh, don't worry. I'm playing dumb on this one. Good thing you never took the bitch's money. You may be the only one who comes out of this smelling like a rose, fuck you very much."

"You're welcome."

"You have supremely bad taste in women."

"I know. Thanks for deleting her."

Deleting her. If only it were that simple.

Adam hung up the phone. No point in staying on the line and incurring more of Fabian's wrath.

In the meantime, he decided to torture himself by turning on the television, to the station he had banned ever since the false reporting of the sexual misconduct claim. Maybe Kirby would show her pretty little lying face on camera.

Instead of Kirby, the grand pooh-bah of false reporting himself graced the screen. But it wasn't the sight of Wainwright's bloated face that made Adam want to fucking throw up. It was the opening lines.

"We've obtained information that the underground club known as The Deep is a probable front for prostitution, where male escorts labeled as 'friends' provide paid-for services to women, upon referral. But the most disturbing plot twist of this sordid tale involves a certain friend named Adam Drake, who was accused of sexual misconduct with a minor a year ago, and who has also been named as the defendant in the theft of two Hermès saddles from his former employer, Becker Farms."

Adam heard only jagged bits and pieces of the rest of it. A bloody hot rage pulsed through his veins and drowned out the rest, as if he'd come down with the highest fever.

He could feel the remnants of his shattered heart, hear the sound of his own labored breaths.

And smell the charred pieces of his pending job offer in Florida.

KIRBY SLAMMED DOWN the cup of hot cocoa that had started to console her.

"No, no, no!" she yelled at Seth's image onscreen. But the little weasel kept talking.

"No charges have been filed on any of the counts, but authorities will soon be conducting a thorough investigation. Meanwhile, Lydia Trussell, owner and general manager of The Deep and its cover club, Deep in the Heart, has not returned our calls…"

Kirby fumbled with her cell phone and misdialed the number of the station before getting it right. The phone practically rattled in her trembling hand as she pressed it to her ear.

None of the extensions answered.

The sweet cocoa-and-marshmallow drink did a U-turn in her stomach, and she fought back the urge to throw up.

Even though her phone had been practically glued to her palm the entire afternoon in the misguided hope Adam would call, she'd somehow missed an email alert from The Deep. Her private session with Adam had been canceled.

She texted him, called him, called the club. She had to convince him she didn't authorize this report, and that she'd deleted what few notes she had. Seth must have bribed the IT department to give him the backup files to her hard drive.

More than anything else, she had to make him understand how much she regretted keeping everything from him. But her entire being felt bruised and battered from hitting so many proverbial brick walls.

No big surprise, The Deep had also locked her out of her portal, so she couldn't send him a private message.

Meanwhile, Baby proceeded to lick her bare feet, but

the puppy only reminded her of her promise to let Adam be the dog's forever home.

Taking care of Baby in the first place meant Reese still owed her a tremendous favor, which gave Kirby one last-resort, certifiably insane idea.

She quickly created a new profile on The Deep's website under Reese's name, then booked the now-open spot that she'd been denied. She dialed her best friend. Thank goodness she answered.

"I need your help, and I need it now," Kirby said, launching right into her plea.

"What happened? Did that guy hurt you? Did something happen to Baby?"

"Baby's okay. It's about how I've hurt 'that guy.' I need you to help me make it right. Are you available tonight?"

"Uh. Yes. But first tell me what I'm getting myself into."

"You're getting into your prettiest dress and putting on your most serious game face. I'll explain everything when I pick you up in an hour."

# 14

ADAM COULDN'T FEEL his legs moving. Every step was a cold and heavy thud. Like the walk of a dead man.

The red-hot rage that had coursed through his veins plummeted into a deep freeze. It might as well have been embalming fluid. At this point, he needed to pretend everything was fine until he could get to the club tonight. If they'd even allow him inside.

He no longer gave a shit what any of them thought, or how Kirby felt. He couldn't imagine screwing someone over as badly as she'd done to him. Not Liv. Not Becker. Instead of lashing out, he'd held in the rage and let it destroy him.

For once in his life, he appreciated having that restraint because he didn't want the one person he cared about to know what had happened. Unless his grandfather already knew.

Adam knocked on the door. No answer.

"Henry?" Adam pounded with more force, all while balancing grocery sacks in each arm.

Even a simple shopping trip took three times longer than usual because every store reminded him of Kirby, and how he had played right into her hands that day.

Finally, his grandfather answered, looking as if he'd been jolted from a nap.

"I told you I could go to the store myself," Henry said.

"And I promised I would bring a few things by before work. At least until we know you're in the clear."

"Well then, come on in. See for yourself. I'm still alive and kicking."

*Glad one of us is*, Adam almost said. But the last thing Henry needed was to be burdened with even more of Adam's problems.

He almost made it to the counter when the bottom fell out of one of the sacks. Canned beans and packaged snacks and everything else spilled across the linoleum. Seemed his life was full of near misses.

More like full-on disasters.

His grandfather surveyed the floor for several seconds before pitching in to put the items on the counter.

"Ritz crackers. Haven't eaten those in years," Henry said as he picked up the box.

Shattered Ritz would be more likely.

"I brought some cheese and peanut butter to go with 'em. Makes for an easy snack. Or even a full meal."

"So that's what you bachelors eat these days?"

A rhetorical question, no doubt. But the question managed to propel Adam's thoughts back to last night. The porterhouse steak for two, complete with the burned edges. The slow dance that bordered on full-body groping. The sex that felt more like lovemaking.

Oh, and the ultimate dessert. Betrayal.

"So, how are things going with your lady friend? Should I get my tuxedo dry-cleaned?"

"Don't bother. We've decided to elope," Adam joked back. But even joking about it wasn't the least bit funny.

"Fix a plate of those crackers, and let's sit down and have a chat."

*Oh, boy. Here it comes.*

Adam fixed an assortment. Some with cheese, some with peanut butter. Most with broken pieces, and a few still intact.

Henry settled into his regular spot on the tapestry-covered sofa.

Adam placed the snacks on the coffee table in front of them.

Ordinarily, he'd take the wingback chair facing the couch. But Henry had an uncanny knack for knowing what was going on without Adam having to say a word, so he settled in next to his grandfather instead. If the man hadn't seen the broadcast, Adam wasn't about to alert him to it. Intentionally or otherwise.

Henry reached for a cracker with cheese and seemed to savor it. "What's going on with you, son?" he asked between bites.

"What do you mean? I'm having this nice dinner with you."

"I mean, what's with all those muscles of yours, and those tattoos?"

*Oh, yeah.* He hadn't even bothered to cover up the one on his biceps this time.

"Ink is in, Henry. We're going to get you a tat for your next birthday."

Henry nodded. "And?"

"And what?"

"Since when did you become a prostitute?"

Damn. Just when he thought this dark cloud would pass by without raining on his already depression-soaked day.

"You saw the broadcast."

"Yes. And I don't believe a word of it."

Against his better judgment, he looked at Henry. He could only imagine how much shame the man would have to endure over this.

"Unfortunately, there is an element of truth to it," Adam admitted. "Where do you want me to start?"

Henry popped the half cracker with peanut butter into his mouth, chewed it slowly, swallowed and brushed the crumbs from his hands.

"Start at the beginning, son. And look me straight in the eye while you're telling it."

By THE TIME Adam finished telling his slightly audited version of the "whole truth and nothing but the truth"—from the part where he covered the Liv tattoo, buffed up to the max and decided to sell his body, mind and soul to women for money, to the part where he was unjustly accused of prostitution and thievery, all in the same broadcast—Henry had wiped the snack plate clean and was staring, blank-faced.

"Well? Say something. This is humiliating enough," Adam said.

"Okay. Why didn't you get the tattoo of Liv's name removed, rather than covering it up with a giant horse's head?"

Now it was Adam's turn to stare. Out of everything he had spilled, and after every sin he'd been publicly accused of committing, that was what concerned his grandfather?

The man cracked a smile.

Adam burst out laughing, then inhaled a soul-cleansing breath and exhaled as thoroughly.

"I wish you would have confided in me sooner," Henry said.

"I already felt like such a failure after the whole Becker incident. Didn't want you to be even more disappointed in me."

"Disappointed? You get to be the shoulder for beautiful, heartbroken women to cry on, and get paid for it? You're my idol."

"Which reminds me," Adam said as he glanced at his watch, "I need to get to the club. But I'll wait until I get there to change. You haven't seen the outfit I have to wear."

"And I probably don't want to, come to think of it."

The atmosphere seemed to stabilize. This was a serious situation, all joking aside. But it already felt easier. Henry knew everything and he was still on Adam's side.

"What's your plan going forward?" Henry asked.

"After I get fired from The Deep? Or after I serve jail time for stealing some saddles that I didn't steal?"

"When and why would you have stolen those saddles? You haven't owned any horses for ten years. Doesn't make sense."

"Exactly. We're not sure what's going on. Bernard wants to sue for defamation. Apparently, in addition to this misinformation now broadcast to four million or so people, the allegation appears in print somewhere. And the Beckers are intent on pressing charges or some sort of bullshit."

"They don't have a case."

"They don't need one. They have an entire legal team. Best of the best. I have Bernard, pro bono. I'm sunk. Suing them will be like throwing rocks at a giant."

"Well, as you know, you only need one well-placed throw."

"True." Except, he wasn't so sure of his aim on this one. Maybe they could blow off the current situation, but

Adam hadn't revealed the actual raunchy depths of the club. Wainwright's broadcast definitely set the stage, but Adam had a feeling more details would come out.

"There's something else you haven't told me, isn't there?" Henry said.

The man was good.

"I probably shouldn't jinx what's left of my life by telling you anything else."

"Not about that. About a certain gal you fixed dinner for the other night. Is there anything you need to talk about?"

*She was a client, and I fucked her. And she fucked me over.*

Still, he couldn't bear to tell Henry the most humiliating part of it. Or, how he had absolutely no intention of looking for a nice girl because he couldn't spot one to save his life.

"Let's just say, it was over before it began."

"Why? Did you serve her the packaged hearts of Romaine instead of the iceberg?"

"I bought the head of iceberg. I wanted to stack the odds in my favor."

That made Henry smile. And it made Adam cringe. That beautiful head of lettuce was still sitting in the crisper.

"You didn't get around to salad, did you?" his grandfather said.

"Not a bite, Henry. Not a bite."


"This is crazy. We could get killed," Reese said.

Kirby pulled into the parking lot, short of the valet, and let her car idle while she talked her friend down from the ledge.

"Don't be so melodramatic. You're safe, Reese. Let's go over it again."

"Okay. You go first."

"No. I have to know you memorized the drill. I'll be by your side, right up until you pass through the red door. And I'll be waiting outside the back exit when you're done."

"I think I'm going to throw up."

"No, you're not. Think of this as a rescue mission. Mine. Now walk me through it."

Reese inhaled a deep, shaky breath. "Okay. I present the valet ticket to the guy inside the door, and say 'I have a reservation, and here's my number.' He checks me in, and I go to the red door in the back of the club and punch in my ticket number. From there, I leave you behind and enter the foyer, where I will soon meet my maker."

"No. You'll be greeted by a superhot blond who calls himself Fabian and he'll confirm your identity, take your ticket and lead you to a room where you'll meet Easy Ride."

"Got it. Then I say I need to go to the ladies' room and tell him I'll be right back. I'll go to the exit instead, and you'll be waiting outside. We'll switch places. I'll give you the wig, you'll give me the hat."

"Perfect! Just remember to note the room number so I don't walk in on somebody else."

"Oh. Right. What if I forget?"

"Breathe, Reese. You won't forget. But if you do, I'll figure something out."

"For the record, I don't like this."

"Neither do I. But I have to talk to him."

"Oh, my God. What do I do after I exit? I already forgot."

"Walk around to the front of the building and wait

for me inside, but near the front door. Let one of those cute cowboys buy you a beer. It will take the edge off. After I leave, or more likely get kicked out, I'll retrieve the Volvo."

"What if they don't give you the valet ticket or the keys?"

"Then we'll steal my car." Kirby produced an extra set and dangled them in front of her friend.

Kirby pulled up to the valet, and the two of them got out. She tipped her cowgirl hat to the man taking her car, then slipped the ticket to Reese. Together, they walked into Deep in the Heart.

The young man at the entrance was the same one Kirby had encountered. She turned her back and feigned interest in a stuffed moose head anchored to the wall while Reese checked in and paid their cover charge.

Reese grabbed her arm soon enough, and Kirby took the lead toward the back of the club.

The dance floor reminded her of her first night there, and how Adam had rescued her ticket. Looking into his eyes had jump-started her heart. The events that followed awakened every other inch of her, and she had felt alive and beautiful again.

Tonight promised to be very different.

Reese punched in the numbers and cast a desperate please-don't-make-me-do-this glance at Kirby before disappearing behind the red door.

Kirby swallowed hard, then headed back toward the entrance, past the drunks and dreamers and everyone else who was oblivious to what was happening. If these people had seen the news report, they didn't act like it. They all minded their own business and enjoyed the music. The thought was only mildly comforting.

She allowed a club employee to stamp her hand for

when she returned for Reese, even though she didn't need a stamp for where she was headed. She needed a guardian angel.

ADAM STOOD IN front of the fireplace in the back room. Although he had banned the reruns of Kirby's first night there, they replayed in his mind anyway. Only this time, he could clearly see the agenda she had brought inside with her.

But that was the past, and he'd never let another woman inside his heart again. Ever.

One appointment down, three to go. Then he could go home to his empty house.

No refunds tonight. No rule-breaking, either, personal or otherwise, even though this might be his last opportunity. No doubt Lydia would decide to cut him loose. At least Wild Indigo would be making their decision by tomorrow. That was something to potentially get excited about.

Except the news report had pretty much rendered him impotent—physically and emotionally. He had no desire for much of anything now, including listening to a bunch of sob stories about love gone wrong. Hell, no one could top his latest story anyway.

"Your eight o'clock is here. I put her in room three," Fabian said.

So formal. By now, they all knew about the news report, and all of them were on their best and most professional behavior. Everyone's required uniform—a white button-down shirt—stayed buttoned tonight. Even Gentleman John could have passed for a real gentleman.

It wasn't lost on Adam how Kirby had originally booked this time slot, and how she'd been canceled. Deleted.

"What's this one's number?" Adam asked without turning around.

"It's 225. Brand-new customer."

Adam jutted his shoulders back, walked to room three and opened the door.

An attractive young woman sat on the sofa. She looked appropriately nervous.

He eased in beside her.

Her skin was pale, her stare was penetrating. Her breathing, labored. It almost looked as if she were about to hurl.

"Hey there. I'm Easy Ride, but everyone calls me Ride."

Every time that bullshit came out of his mouth, he nearly gagged on it. But first names were definitely out of the question. At least Seth-the-Prick Wainwright hadn't revealed Adam's moniker. An odd and less-than-thorough oversight.

"Hi, Ride. Um. Is there any chance I can go to the ladies' room before we get started?"

Of course, half of them made the same request. And half of those came back properly freshened up, for whatever reason. As if they needed to impress a prostitute.

Pathetic. Every last one of them. Himself included.

He felt a chuckle rise in his throat, but he managed to swallow it back long enough to say, "It's right down the hall. Next to the exit."

"You'll wait here for me?"

Her nervousness was rather sweet. He could relate to the fragility. Despite her angelic beauty, he felt absolutely nothing for this person. No attraction on any level. No desire to rip off her dress or hear her out.

Nothing.

Feigning interest and getting through this evening was going to be harder than he had originally thought.

"I'll wait right here. Take as long as you need."

As soon as the door shut behind her, he whispered under his breath, "Hell, take the whole hour. Please."

She really was taking quite a while, Adam noticed after about ten minutes had passed. Maybe at least one of his wishes would come true. He turned on the sound system, changing the station from the country Muzak to real country rock.

He stood, stretched his legs and removed his hat. When he turned back around, she had returned. Only, it wasn't the same woman who had left.

Even with the stupid wig, there was no disguising her.

"Please, don't kick me out. I need to talk to you," Kirby said.

He looked at her with such anger, but there was more. Hurt. Betrayal.

She shed the wig and walked toward him. She wanted to touch him. Needed to feel his skin.

"Sit," he demanded.

She didn't dare argue. Rather, she was grateful he hadn't thrown her out with his own hands.

"You need a shoulder to cry on, baby? Oh, wait, you want something really good to write about, don't you?" he said.

Before she could formulate a response, he cranked up the music, then proceeded to unbutton and completely shed his shirt.

"I'm not here for a story. I need to tell you some things," she said in a raised voice, trying to be heard over the music.

He didn't acknowledge whether he'd heard. Instead, he continued to remove his belt.

She gulped. Hard.

"Seth confiscated my notes. I wasn't going to air anything about you, but I did find out some things you need to know," she called out. "Please, I want to talk."

As he unbuttoned the top button of his jeans, her sex pulsed and contracted against her will, against her common sense.

"Is that what you want? To talk? Well, I'm the host. You'll graciously accept what I offer," he said, mocking her words from the previous night.

He firmly eased her down to her back, and she swore he was about to kiss her, which was beyond crazy because she would have let him. She wanted to kiss him, still. Instead, he proceeded to straddle her chest.

He moved his hips in slow and sensual strokes to the beat of the music. The way he'd moved with her last night. The way he obviously knew she liked.

All of a sudden, she felt flushed and red from the inside out as she tried to digest the uneasy cocktail of excitement and confusion.

And embarrassment.

Embarrassment over opening her mouth to him, willingly and eagerly spreading her legs so wide she thought she would break, allowing him to make love to a woman who'd harbored ulterior motives.

In all the whirl of movement, and much-too-loud music, she managed to grab one of his arms and tug him down. It took every ounce of strength she could manage, but it was as if her need to rectify this was stronger than his ill feelings toward her now.

He settled on top of her as he had that first night, nudged her legs apart with his own and pressed into her.

He grew harder against her. He still wanted her, even through the anger. His body couldn't lie.

Neither could hers.

Her mouth wasn't willing to lie anymore, either. But he wouldn't allow her to talk.

Instead, he began kissing her with an intensity that took her breath away. Even though she didn't want it to happen like this, she didn't fight it.

He began to thrust his hips against her, to the slow, steady pulsing beat of the song. Turning her on while simultaneously confusing the hell out of her, and all she could think was: *this is better than being ignored. This is better than being rejected.*

But it wasn't better than what they almost had.

As swiftly as the song ended, he stood.

"Your time is up. Report whatever you want. Just get out," he said as he rebuttoned his jeans.

"Let me explain everything."

"Leave."

"No."

"Then let me guess. You're sorry that it ever went this far."

"I should have told you the truth earlier. I wanted to, but I didn't know how."

"You had every opportunity to tell me the truth." He jerked his shirt back on and proceeded to button it.

"I'm sorry about the way I handled it. I—"

"You're sorry, all right. No wonder your husband didn't want you."

*What?*

The words seemed to hang between them for an eternity...*didn't want you. No wonder.*

He opened his mouth as if he wanted to either take

back what had already been said, or say even more. Instead, he stormed out the door.

There was nothing else to say anyway. He'd used her most painful confession against her.

After the initial humiliation and soul-draining agony of it, an odd numbness settled in. All the confusion and pain and embarrassment condensed to a clearly defined point, where there was no longer any question, only complete understanding. A pure, undeniable truth.

It was over between them.

And they both knew it.

# 15

KIRBY HAD STAYED up all night, polishing her pitch along with a backup plan.

She marched into Bettencourt's office this time and closed the door behind her but remained standing.

Bettencourt looked up and didn't miss a beat. "I'm sorry Seth presented your story instead of waiting for you."

She started to speak, but he interrupted.

"There was chatter that another station had been tipped off. We had to air it first. Sure enough, Channel 2 aired a similar story last night. Your guy wasn't mentioned in theirs, so we're ahead of the game. Now, I know what you're thinking, Kirby, but I had to let Seth proceed with the information he had. I'm sure you understand my position."

She wanted to scream at the top of her lungs that this was exactly the type of scenario she had tried to avoid. Thank God she hadn't downloaded the video on her work computer. Not that it proved anything, but Seth would have eagerly tried to spin it that way.

She remained composed, even though she hadn't even consumed her usual four mugs of coffee, and was operating on little sleep. The thought of Adam was providing the adrenaline.

"I'm not upset. But, for the record, there's no basis for the earlier sexual allegations against Adam Drake, and no wrongdoing on his behalf in the case of the missing Hermès saddles, as Seth had reported. These misstatements need to be corrected. Since he aired the story that was supposed to be mine, I'd like to air those retractions, along with some additional information about the club that wasn't documented."

Bettencourt shifted in his seat.

"You can't directly contradict his report. Especially when he got that impression from your research. If you're worried that you've lost your only chance, you haven't. I'll give you a shot at the oil-and-gas scandal. You have a bright future here."

If only she'd traded stories with Seth from the beginning, none of this would have happened. She also wouldn't have met Adam.

"I appreciate that, but I thought we were all about telling the truth."

"Kirby, you know the truth about your contact better than anyone, and I believe you. We'll talk about a retraction later. You mentioned other information. What else do you have?"

*Besides the truth?* That was why she'd wanted to be a reporter in the first place, but now she was being asked to withhold it. And withholding, in any form, was unacceptable.

She gripped the piece of paper and contemplated her next move. Ironically enough, her backup plan had little to do with truths of any kind.

"I dug deep, like you instructed. Since I can't issue

a retraction, I'd like to go live with this." She handed him the paper.

While he reviewed the content, she unclipped her cell phone from her waist and forwarded the footage to the part where she and Adam were deep in the throes. With a shaky thumb, she put it on Pause and waited for Bettencourt to finish.

"Orgies? Sex toys being passed around without proper sanitation?" he said. His entire upper body visibly quivered.

Kirby nodded, then snatched the paper from his hand.

"If for any reason Seth steals this out from under me, I'll deny everything, and I'll give Channel 2 exclusive rights to the things I did not include. I left out the juiciest part on purpose. I want to be the one to bring down The Deep, and I want to do it tonight. I'm sure you understand *my* position."

Bettencourt seemed to contemplate it, if only because she'd forced him to do so.

"You sure you want to do this? It's your reputation, as well."

"Don't worry about my reputation. I'm not. In fact, I have some footage I'd be willing to air, in support of my narrative."

She turned the phone around and willed her hand to stop shaking long enough to bait him.

Listening to the audio alone was torturous. Fortunately, the video quality was poor enough to raise questions as to what, exactly, the two of them were doing on that sofa.

When Bettencourt had obviously seen enough, she turned off the phone.

He cleared his throat. "I appreciate your willingness to go all the way, so to speak, to get the story. But let's leave out the footage, in case young children are watching. You have my permission to go on air with the information you've presented, as long as you don't use any words or descriptions that would land us in hot water."

"Thank you. And, for the record, let's not pretend Seth didn't take advantage of my absence for his own gain."

Bettencourt simply stared in response to her straightforwardness. But she couldn't leave without it being said.

Now she needed to shred this fake script and stash her personal belongings in her car before she went to Deep in the Heart for the on-location segment because, in all likelihood, she wouldn't be allowed back on these premises.

Seth glanced up as she passed by.

Instead of giving him the finger, she gave him the thumbs-up. She took her time for the full effect.

Predictably enough, Seth walked over, sans his confident wobble.

"So, you're not mad at me?" he asked.

"Why would I be? I didn't feel well. Besides, you did me a favor."

"I'm relieved. I'm also a bit surprised."

Suspicious was more like it.

"Don't be. You were right. I wavered. Besides, you paved the way for me to embellish. I'll be live at five."

She looked at him the moment her words hit.

"You're bullshitting me."

"No, sir."

"You have more information? Why didn't you document it?"

"I didn't know you were going to steal my notes, or I would have been more thorough." She chased the sarcasm with a huge grin.

He turned on his heel and headed straight to Betten-court's office.

For once, she wasn't the least bit concerned.

She spent the rest of the day backing her files to a flash drive, contacting the other media outlets in Houston to give them a heads-up about her segment and arranging a one-on-one with the Houston Police Department to go over everything she knew about the false allegations against Adam.

After she'd finished all necessary covert housecleaning, she retrieved the actual script she planned to use and headed to the club.

She'd wanted to get everything she needed to say on paper, although these particular truths could easily be spoken from the heart. She wouldn't need a script to thank Adam for wanting her, if only for a while. Even though the two of them didn't have a future together, he'd rescued her from the prison of her own past. No matter what happened from here, she'd finally be able to look at herself in the mirror, like the person she saw, and genuinely love the person she intended on becoming.

"You're on in five," an assistant said the minute Kirby got out of her car and caught up with the camera crew.

The afternoon had passed by so fast. Life passed by so fast. Even the drive from the station passed by in a jagged heartbeat.

Two other stations were set up for broadcast. Word had spread.

The cameraman assumed his position, legs anchored to the ground, camera resting on his shoulder.

The audio guy nodded, then held up five fingers and paused.

A flurry of butterflies and wasps swarmed in her

gut. What she was about to do was both beautiful and terrifying.

*Four...*

She cleared her throat, willed her hands to stop shaking and straightened the collar of the white shirt Adam had left behind. It still smelled of pine and vanilla.

*Three...*

Both of her horseshoe earrings dangled, unobstructed, against her trembling jaw.

*Two...*

This was it. Her first on-air broadcast. It would also be her last.

*One.*

ADAM COULD ALWAYS count on Fabian to rescue him.

If it hadn't been for his friend's insistence that Adam meet him at the Western Pleasure Saloon for a drink, Adam would have probably disappeared down a familiar black hole of depression. One that he'd dug for himself when he said words he never would have otherwise said.

*No wonder your husband didn't want you.*

No matter what Kirby had done—and she had arguably done the worst thing possible, short of cheating on him—he wouldn't want to crush her that way. Wouldn't, but had. And it wasn't even the fucking truth. He never for one second thought Kirby did anything to deserve such rejection. Maybe someday, if his life were ever in a better place, he'd tell her that much.

He could definitely use a drink or three, and he had plenty of time to nurse every bottle that lined the shelves across the whole bar. Yep, plenty of time, since Lydia had put him on suspension, which mercifully shifted his thoughts to his other problem. Unemployment.

The thought of what went on in the club, and how he

never broke the cardinal rule but was the one who had to leave, tickled the hell out of him. Life didn't get any damn funnier, he mused as he downed half a Dos Equis without coming up for air.

Gentleman John and Cowboy Roy eyed him from a few seats down. John even shrugged as if to say, "Tough luck, Ride."

Little did any of the guys know that Adam's tough luck was contagious. Their days were numbered at the club, as well. Lydia might have put him on suspension, but she also told him about her plans to lock the red door for good, do some major housecleaning and focus on the legitimate end of the business after the dust settled. That was, assuming she didn't get charged with running a brothel.

He hadn't seen the other reports, but he'd heard about the story airing on at least one other channel. That station didn't implicate him, so maybe Bernard could pull something from the ashes.

The bartender placed two more longnecks on the bar. One for him, and one for Fabian.

"You're a hell of a mind reader, Joe," Adam said as he reached into his pocket to pay.

Joe quickly knocked it back. "On the house," he insisted.

"I can spot you some cash, if you need it at some point," Fabian said.

"Can you spot me a place on your sofa? Might be cheaper than my house note."

"Anytime, my friend."

No everything-will-turn-out-fine bullshit tonight. And no more calling him Ride, which was more than fine.

The sixty-inch flat-screen television over the bar competed with the drunken conversations among patrons, and damn if it wasn't on Channel 53. Any minute now, that lowlife reporter Seth Wainwright would rear his ugly face and body. And equally ugly ethics.

At that point, any and all beers Adam had consumed would be redeposited on top of the bar.

He was halfway curious to find out what new crime he'd committed, because he was always the last to know. The other half wanted to down as much beer as he could, and keep it down.

"Hey, change the station," Adam called out to Joe.

"No can do. The owner says it needs to stay put on this one."

"I'll pay you," Adam said.

For a split second, Adam's world began to literally spin. Then he realized Fabian was spinning his bar stool around to where he wouldn't be facing the screen.

"Thanks," Adam said as he finished off longneck number two. The icy cold liquid felt good on his throat.

"No fucking way," Fabian said.

Adam swirled back around.

Kirby, of all people, live on location. Was that his shirt she was wearing? Sure as hell looked like it.

All the anger and regret and confusion rose from his stomach to his throat. He gulped back the urgent need to hurl, while the other guys hollered and booed.

Gentleman John threw some trail mix at the screen, and the guys burst out laughing when it hit the bull's-eye. Right in the forehead.

*All you need is one good throw...*

Adam hoisted himself onto the bar and cranked up the volume.

"Hey, Ride, you're blocking the view," Cowboy Roy called out.

Being that close to Kirby's gorgeous, lying, wounded face wasn't a place he needed to be anyway, so he stepped aside.

"...standing here in front of Deep in the Heart where, yesterday afternoon, Seth Wainwright aired lies with regard to the inner-sanctum establishment called The Deep. I know, because I'm the one who investigated. At no time did money change hands between Adam Drake and myself. And I possess no proof that money was exchanged between any of the other clients and employees for sex-related services.

"Since I will likely be fired on the spot, please check my blog, where I will be writing a series of reports on my own investigation into an even more important story—the wrongful accusations of theft against Mr. Drake by his former employer, Becker Farms. As far as the previous accusations for sexual misconduct, I've spoken with the accuser, who has recanted her version of events, and I've linked the theft of the Hermès saddles to that same accuser. Over the next several months, I'll be working directly with the HPD and various media outlets. Again, please check my blog. And Adam, if you're watching, I—"

The screen went dark. Moments later, a commercial aired, followed by a disclaimer by the news director.

The whole bar exploded with hoots and hollers of a different kind this time. But it paled in comparison to what Adam felt at the moment.

His cell phone vibrated in his pocket. He hoped to find a text from Kirby, finishing what she was about to say because even though he was confused and grateful and maybe still a little mad, he was ready to hear the end of that last sentence.

Turned out, only one text had come through. And it wasn't from her.

If he hadn't been in a bar full of testosterone, he probably would have fucking cried. His dream job in Florida was being offered up on a digital platter. The text simply read, Welcome aboard, Mr. Drake. How soon can you start?

His thoughts flitted to so many places before finding their way back home, and his heart must have skipped multiple beats before deciding what it wanted. Really wanted.

*Start.* He definitely wanted to start right away. As in, start a new chapter in his life. One where he didn't have to hide, didn't have to feel unwanted and unloved and ashamed. One where the truth eventually prevailed, and where people forfeited their own dreams to reveal it. Yes, he wanted that more than anything.

Furthermore, he knew exactly where to find it.

# 16

Kirby fumbled with the keys to her loft as her cell phone alerted her to another text, another voice mail, another email.

Bettencourt had left one voice mail. Seth had left none. No doubt the weasel was hacking into her computer backup records, trying to come up with a way to discredit her.

Reese sent one text. It read: OMG. That was awesome!!!

Nothing from Adam. Not that she expected anything. Hopefully, she did more good than harm.

This whole thing had taken such a toll on her. She'd only now stopped to allow Adam's last words to sink in.

*No wonder your husband didn't want you.*

Yet, she'd learned to read Adam. She'd watched his expression when he'd said those words. He didn't mean them.

Or maybe she simply didn't want to believe he meant them.

Oh, well. She had lived without true love and passion for a long time. She'd survive without it again.

Finally, she got the key in the damn lock.

Baby greeted her with unbridled enthusiasm, then waited by the door long after she closed it.

*Even Baby wants to leave me.*

She quickly reined in the thought. She knew what the puppy wanted. Make that, whom she wanted.

"Don't hold your breath, Baby. He's not coming back."

She dropped the weighed-down purse on the floor. It didn't contain any souvenirs from the station. Only the photo she had kept on her desk of Lady, enshrined in a crystal frame.

Lady waited patiently by her bowl as Kirby positioned the picture on the bookshelf, filling the space left by the Christmas party photo, which was still face-down on the counter.

She went to the kitchen, yanked the troublemaker from its frame, held it over the sink and lit a match.

Burned edges. She still loved 'em.

Hopefully, the smoke wouldn't set off the alarm. Last thing she needed tonight was more drama.

Baby's needs suddenly became immediate. She had remained by the front door and was now barking, which meant she needed to go outside and take care of some business. Judging by the volume and frequency of Baby's barks, the business could be huge.

Kirby offered Lady a treat to tide her over, then quickly leashed Baby and opened the door. But her path was blocked.

Baby transformed from impatient to deliriously happy.

Kirby's reaction was a bit more reserved. She couldn't read anything in Adam's eyes.

"I'm here for Baby," he said. "You promised."

Yes. She had promised.

Either he hadn't seen the broadcast, or it hadn't made a difference.

She handed over the leash, and it felt as if she'd lost part of herself. At least she knew Baby would have a good home. A great home, actually, with lots of square footage, both indoor and outdoor. Or maybe she'd end up being a beach baby in Florida.

She dared to look at Adam one more time.

"Wait there for a minute, if you don't mind," she said. "I'll put her toys in a sack. They mean a lot to her."

She headed to the area rug, where a few of Baby's toys were scattered, but the door shut behind her. Although it wasn't loud, it still knocked the breath out of her with its implication. *He left.*

She whipped around, only to find he had come inside instead.

After placing the toys in a paper grocery sack, she surrendered it, along with any hope of reconciliation.

"What was it you wanted to say?" he asked.

She inventoried her thoughts. What hadn't she already said, or tried to say at the club last night? But the music had been too loud. And he'd been unwilling to hear.

He seemed ready to hear now, but the news story had depleted her. She didn't have the energy to repeat it, only to be called a liar again.

She, quite simply, had no fight left within her.

"I've said everything I need to say. I guess you didn't hear it."

"I didn't hear it because the broadcast cut to commercial."

He moved closer. So close she could smell the barley and hops on his breath, along with a hint of Dentyne. So close she could feel his body heat, even from beneath his tight black T-shirt.

So close she could practically hear his heart beating as fast as hers. Now, she understood the question completely.

"I—I don't remember."

She couldn't look him in the eye. Couldn't say directly to him what she was so eager to admit in front of four million people.

"Say it, Kirby. If it's what I think it is, I promise to say it back."

She looked at his eyes now. They had softened to the baby blue she loved.

"I said, 'Adam, if you're listening, I really did love you.' And I still do." Tears welled up in her eyes, and she willed the floodgates to hold them in.

Instead of saying a word, he turned around and opened the door with Baby in tow.

"Oh. I see," she said. "You're leaving now. Without saying it back. I know I deserve it. I had just hoped—"

"I'm taking Baby outside. I can tell she needs to go real bad. I'll be right back for the other baby I came here to claim. And to tell her I love her, too. I never stopped."

He winked, and then disappeared down the hall. The clap of his boots kept up with the scramble of the tiny paws that led the way while Kirby stood perfectly still. As if it would all disappear if she dared to breathe.

A STREAM OF morning light roused Adam from his sleep like a warm, loving touch.

Kirby was still asleep beside him. One of those crazy horseshoe earrings of hers had survived the night. The other one rested on the pillow next to her silky brown hair.

He plucked the stray earring from the pillow and contemplated its power. Maybe these things really did work.

Kirby's soft snore sounded like a purr now. Only, on closer inspection, the purr had to be coming from her beautiful black cat, who was curled up on the opposite side of Kirby.

Damn if he didn't want to nudge Kirby awake and make her purr, as well.

Maybe in a minute. They'd exhausted apologies and explanations, and he felt pretty sure he had convinced her that he didn't mean to say what he had said at the club. Although he'd gladly keep reminding her how much he wanted her. Always did. Always would.

They'd bathed each other in compliments and I-love-yous. They'd kissed each other to sleep. Their tongues had danced, taking turns leading. Their bodies had remained simply yet erotically entwined beneath the soft comforter, braided together like the strongest velvet rope as he focused exclusively on the softness of her mouth. In many ways, it was the best sex he'd ever had.

He quietly chuckled. He must really have it bad for her if cuddling and kissing alone did it for him.

He walked into the kitchen area and retrieved his cell phone. The tremendous backlog of texts and voice mails winked back, as if they knew he'd been busy and would patiently wait for his return.

Most of the texts were from Fabian, but his attorney had authored a few. Lydia had left one, as well. He'd also received several hang-ups and two voice messages. No way he'd ever forget either number, but one of them he'd love to forget altogether. Becker Farms.

No doubt they'd seen the broadcast. If they hadn't, he'd gladly burn it to DVD and overnight a copy to them. After all, burning things was what he did best.

Even if they begged him to come back, he'd have to

think long and hard about it. Not that that would happen, but he'd love the opportunity to turn them down.

He smiled when he thought of what Kirby had ultimately sacrificed, and how they were both out of a job.

*We might have to move in together*, he concluded. *Save money. Live off love.*

Maybe being unemployed for a little longer wouldn't be so bad after all.

Lydia's text offered Adam a chance to come back and work at the proper club, Deep in the Heart, maybe as a bartender or front-door man.

This one was easy. He punched in Thanks, but no thanks. Best of luck to you and the guys, and sent it without pause or regret. He liked Lydia, but he liked Kirby a whole lot more.

*Loved.*

He played the voice message from Henry next. "I saw the person I assume to be your girlfriend on television. She's a beauty. Seems like a good person, when it counts the most. I vote we hang around H-town a little longer. Just sayin'."

Yes, Henry was just sayin' that maybe his own wish was about to come true.

Marriage wasn't something Adam had considered, but he definitely wasn't ruling it out. He could picture telling a G-rated version of this story to his kids, and his own grandkids.

*Our own grandkids.*

He shook his head at the bold and much-too-forward thought. He really needed to find a way to support himself first, before he started making babies.

Which reminded him, he owed Wild Indigo a response. He typed, I apologize, but I have to decline.

I've been presented with an opportunity in Houston that I simply can't turn down. Thank you, again, for considering me for such a prestigious position.

As soon as he pressed Send, he considered how he could have perhaps taken the job and asked Kirby to go with him. They could have escaped their mutual pasts together. Yet, confronting his past seemed like a better idea, and he was ready to help Kirby in any way he could.

He turned his phone off completely and walked back into the bedroom, only to find Kirby gone. He called her name and looked around her loft. All six hundred or so square feet of it.

"Kirby? Where are you hiding?" he called out.

"I'm right here. Behind you," she said. "One-hundred percent."

Before he could turn, she wrapped her arms around his waist and pressed fully against his bare back.

She ran her fingertip up his arm and around the edges of his tattoo, then seemed to trace the letters that had been inked over. He'd all but forgotten about the thing. Mainly about how it didn't bother him the least bit anymore, except he never told Kirby the story behind it.

"I should get that removed," he said.

"Don't you dare. It's perfect the way it is. In fact, I was thinking of getting one, as well. Except mine would say 'Easy Ride.'"

"Don't know the person. It's definitely not me. Not anymore."

"Then I guess it will stand for the hot guy who brought us together."

He turned around.

There she stood. Dressed in his white unbuttoned

shirt and nothing else. His cock twitched as he parted the halves and took in her exquisite form.

"I don't want any ink touching that flawless body of yours."

"Hmm. Well, my body is craving to be touched. What are my options?"

His grin spread. Options? Yeah, he had plenty of those. And plenty of time to fulfill them.

Kirby led him back to the bedroom and sat on the edge of the bed.

He started to kneel. Damn if he wasn't starving at the sight of her.

"Stand," she said. "You promised me something."

"I told you I love you, but if you insist on hearing it again, I love you. Now, will you please let me show it?"

"Not that promise. The other one."

He racked his freakin' brain. They'd pretty much exhausted all topics, revealed all the secrets.

"I give up," he finally said.

But then that gorgeous, drop-dead smile crossed her face. And he remembered.

In one night, everything wrong about Kirby's life had been made right.

She could taste him in her mouth, and smell him on her skin. She could still feel his hardness pressing into her soft palate, and his silky texture against her lips.

"Did you…?" he began, but stopped.

Did she ever. Even thinking about it caused a serious contraction deep within. Instead of answering, she took his hand and pressed it between her legs. Her body couldn't lie.

His grin confirmed that he understood what she wasn't saying.

"I know this will sound strange," he said. "But I can't wait to tell Henry about this."

"That I gave you a blow job? Or that I came while giving it to you?"

He laughed a deep, hearty laugh. "No. I'm going to tell him I met a nice girl who's naughty in all the right ways. And that we'll probably be panhandling soon, so if he drives by, please toss us some coins."

It was her turn to laugh, because the only other option was to cry. And crying was something she'd definitely pass on.

"I have a feeling things will eventually go our way," she said.

"I don't know how you know these things, but somehow you do."

"I have a secret weapon."

"I think we should agree to have no more secret anythings."

"You're right. So I'll officially surrender mine. I can read the inflections in your voice, and I can tell whether you're telling the truth."

"I'm not scared. I don't plan to lie to you or keep anything from you. Ever again. Which means I better fess up about the tattoo on my bicep."

"No need. I know it covers the name of your ex. And I do believe that tattoo was your downfall."

He had to smile. "Of course you know. But why do you think it was my downfall? Besides the obvious. I fell for the wrong girl."

"Because an even worse girl got jealous over your ink, and made up adult lies to tell about you."

"Is that what Madison said?"

Kirby nodded. "Oops. I do have one more confession. Not really a confession. But I did withhold some information."

Judging by his heavy sigh, perhaps she shouldn't have waited.

"I'm only telling you this because apparently you didn't play your voice mail from Trish and Donald Becker," she continued.

"You knew about that? Please tell me you weren't snooping again."

She sat up straight. "I resent that, but I forgive you. The two of them called me after the broadcast. I'd told Trish about what Madison confessed, but neither of them knew I'd connected her to the missing saddles."

"I still don't get how that happened. Unless…"

Obviously, it was his turn to fill in the missing information. Specifically, how did Madison get into the vault?

"Did she somehow take your keys when you weren't looking?"

Adam shook his head. "No. I don't see how. But her trainer borrowed them once."

"While Madison was there?"

"Quite possibly."

"Impressive deduction. Maybe you should be an investigative reporter." She eased back down beside him.

"No, thanks. One reporter in the family is plenty. What else did the Beckers say?"

"They said they'd call you next and apologize immediately. I told them the universe was running a special on forgiveness and second chances at the moment, but they better hurry."

"I'm sorry I suspected you of snooping," he said.

"You can make it up to me by listening to the Beckers' offer. They want you back."

"I don't know, Kirby."

She snuggled closer now and placed her arm across his warm chest.

"I don't blame you. If I were you, I wouldn't be persuaded by an offer to double my previous salary."

"I'm not," he said a little too confidently. "In fact, I'm offended by it."

Adam eased out from under her arm and stood.

"Stay," he said.

There he went, totally nude and gorgeous every step of the way. And he was all hers.

She strained to hear what he was saying, obviously to one Becker or the other. But she vowed never to snoop or eavesdrop again. It had almost cost her everything.

When he came back into the room, his expression gave away nothing short of complete satisfaction.

"You told Mr. Becker off, didn't you," she said.

Adam crawled beneath the covers and embraced her.

"Remember my telling you about a job possibility in Florida? Wild Indigo Equestrian Center. Golden opportunity. They texted the offer last night," he said, effectively dodging her question.

"You're moving? To Florida?"

At that, her heart sank. What did that mean for her? For them?

"Not a chance," he said.

"How come?"

"Why would I follow a golden opportunity when I have a platinum one right here?" He touched the end of her nose with the pad of his index finger.

"You'd turn down a fabulous job offer for me?"

She looked into those baby blues. And those baby blues looked into her. But then the reality of it hit her. "Oh, no. You told off Becker."

"Yes, I did. I told him that his offer was offensive, and I want nothing less than part ownership. I want full ownership of Daisy and the corgi, Sergeant, and I want part of the adjacent land that he owns. You and I can open an animal rescue sanctuary. I'd need for you to run it, of course, and he'd have to pay you a nice salary."

The whole thing blew her away. Animal rescue sanctuary? Talk about a dream come true. Even better than becoming an investigative reporter. In fact, this opportunity was pure platinum.

And Adam thought of it. For her.

"Well? What did he say?"

"He said 'no.'"

She swallowed back her disappointment, for Adam's sake. No matter. Her most important dream had already been realized. Adam was there. With her.

"Hey, you tried. I'm proud of you. We'll figure out something else. Together."

"You didn't let me finish. He said 'no' to paying you a salary. That would have to come out of my part of the ownership."

She'd only thought she couldn't be any happier, but he just took her there.

"So, you would be my boss?" she asked.

"Let's pretend it would make me your client."

"Oh, yeah? In that case, we'll have to make some rules."

"As long as they're breakable," he said.

He proceeded to kiss her tentatively at first, then deeper, taking her back to that first day in the club, where she'd opened her soul enough to let him inside. Where she'd learned that broken hearts could heal, and good intentions could be shattered but mended because the past, with all its heaviness, couldn't outrun the future—especially not when the future was as honest and promising and tempting as...*this*.

\* \* \* \* \*

**Harlequin is thrilled to announce
the launch of a new sexy, contemporary
digital-only series in January 2018!
With the exciting launch of this new
series, June 2017 will be the last month of
publication for Harlequin® Blaze® books.**

For more passionate stories, indulge in these fun,
sexy reads with the irresistible heroes you can't
get enough of!

**HARLEQUIN** *Presents.*

Glamorous international settings…
powerful men…passionate romances.

**HARLEQUIN** *Desire*

Powerful heroes…scandalous secrets…
burning desires.

HBEND0617

# If you enjoy passionate stories from Harlequin® Blaze®, you will love Harlequin® Presents!

Do you want alpha males, decadent glamour and jet-set lifestyles? Step into the sensational, sophisticated world of Harlequin® Presents, where sinfully tempting heroes ignite a fierce and wickedly irresistible passion!

**Look for eight new stories every month!**
**Recommended Read for July 2017**

Maisey Yates The Prince's Captive Virgin Ruthless prince Adam Katsaros offers Belle a deal—he'll release her father if she becomes his mistress! Adam's gaze awakens a heated desire in Belle. Her innocent beauty might redeem his royal reputation—but can she tame the beast inside?

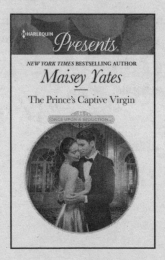

# Look out for The Secret Billionaires trilogy from Harlequin® Presents!

**Three extraordinary men accept the challenge of leaving their billionaire lifestyles behind. But in *Salazar's One-Night Heir* by Jennifer Hayward, Alejandro must also seek revenge for a decades-old injustice…**

Tycoon Alejandro Salazar will take any opportunity to expose the Hargrove family's crime against his—including accepting a challenge to pose as their stable groom! His goal in sight, Alejandro cannot allow himself to be distracted by the gorgeous Hargrove heiress…

Her family must pay, yet Alejandro can't resist innocent Cecily's fiery passion. And when their one night of bliss results in an unexpected pregnancy, Alejandro will legitimize his heir and restore his family's honor…by binding Cecily to him with a diamond ring!

Don't miss

## The Secret Billionaires
# *SALAZAR'S ONE-NIGHT HEIR*

**by Jennifer Hayward Available July 2017!**

HP0620172

*Ariston Kavakos makes impoverished Keeley Turner a
proposition: a month's employment on his island, at his
command. Soon her resistance to their sizzling chemistry
weakens! But when there's a consequence, Ariston makes
one thing clear: Keeley will become his bride…*

Read on for a sneak preview of
### Sharon Kendrick's book
### THE PREGNANT KAVAKOS BRIDE

***ONE NIGHT WITH CONSEQUENCES***
*Conveniently wedded, passionately bedded!*

"You're offering to buy my baby? Are you out of your
mind?"

"I'm giving you the opportunity to make a fresh start."

"Without my baby?"

"A baby will tie you down. I can give this child everything
it needs," Ariston said, deliberately allowing his gaze to drift
around the dingy little room. "You cannot."

"Oh, but that's where you're wrong, Ariston," Keeley
said, her hands clenching. "You might have all the houses
and yachts and servants in the world, but you have a great
big hole where your heart should be—and therefore you're
incapable of giving this child the thing it needs more than
anything else!"

"Which is?"

"Love!"

Ariston felt his body stiffen. He loved his brother
and once he'd loved his mother, but he was aware of his
limitations. No, he didn't do the big showy emotion he

suspected she was talking about, and why should he, when he knew the brutal heartache it could cause? Yet something told him that trying to defend his own position was pointless. She would fight for this child, he realized. She would fight with all the strength she possessed, and that was going to complicate things. Did she imagine he was going to accept what she'd just told him and play no part in it? Politely dole out payments and have sporadic weekend meetings with his own flesh and blood? Or worse, no meetings at all? He met the green blaze of her eyes.

"So you won't give this baby up and neither will I," he said softly. "Which means that the only solution is for me to marry you."

He saw the shock and horror on her face.

"But I don't want to marry you! It wouldn't work, Ariston—on so many levels. You must realize that. Me, as the wife of an autocratic control freak who doesn't even like me? I don't think so."

"It wasn't a question," he said silkily. "It was a statement. It's not a case of if you will marry me, Keeley—just when."

"You're mad," she breathed.

He shook his head. "Just determined to get what is rightfully mine. So why not consider what I've said, and sleep on it and I'll return tomorrow at noon for your answer—when you've calmed down. But I'm warning you now, Keeley—that if you are willful enough to try to refuse me, or if you make some foolish attempt to run away and escape—" he paused and looked straight into her eyes "—I will find you and drag you through every court in the land to get what is rightfully mine."

*Don't miss*
*THE PREGNANT KAVAKOS BRIDE*
*available July 2017 wherever*
*Harlequin Presents® books and ebooks are sold.*

www.Harlequin.com